Dark Streets and the Forgotten Tastes of Chocolate and Joy
An urban fantasy collection

Jennifer Rachel Baumer

Monstrosity Ink
Reno, Nevada

**Dark Streets and the Forgotten Tastes
of Chocolate and Joy
An urban fantasy collection**

Copyright © 2014 by Jennifer Rachel Baumer
Published by Monstrosity Ink
Cover art Copyright © 2014 by Jorge Salcedo
Book and cover design copyright © 2014 by Monstrosity Ink

ISBN – 13: 978-0692241189 (Monstrosity Ink)
ISBN – 10: 0692241183

"Autumn Equinox" © 2005
Originally appeared in Playthings of the Gods, Drollerie Press
"City Limits" © 2010
Originally appeared in The Lorelei Signal, Jan-Mar 201
"New & Improved" © 2010
Originally appeared in Retro Spec: Tales of Fantasy and Nostalgia
Raven Eletrick Ink, © 2010
"Custody" © 2005
Originally appeared in Abyss & Apex, Issue #15, 2005
"What We're Going to do Next" © 2003
This story originally appeared in Say… Aren't You Dead?
Issue 3, 2003
"Dark Streets and the Forgotten Tastes of Chocolate and Joy" © 2007
Originally appeared in Jabberwocky, Prime Books
As *"The Forgotten Tastes of Chocolate and Joy"*
"Fishing Line, Feathers & Waffles" © 2006
Originally appeared in Not One of Us, Issue #36, 2006

Monstrosity Ink

Table of Contents

Contents

Greek Mythology has fascinated me since I was a kid watching Hercules cartoons. I read Bulfinch's Mythology in seventh grade and probably wrote my first myth before I got out of high school. High school and myths combine in Autumn Equinox, a cautionary tale about just what money can't buy.

Autumn Equinox

I. Lachesis (The Past)

Echoes of the door slamming. Hours later it would still ring in her head.

Not all of them. Not all the doors. They were all steel core, and there were five they passed through between intake and the holding cell.

Just that first door. Hours later, the sound of it slamming still echoed. Not a sharp sound. A world-ending – what? Not a slam. Not a thud. Not a bang. More like a shattering. As if solid iron had shattered.

The world broken apart.

That door. Painted a very weird sickly skin color. Hard, upraised, textured, nubby. Ice cold. She'd touched it right after the world-ending sound.

They'd told her not to.

"Keep your hands laced behind your back."

"Fuck you. My mother drives a Lexus."

The door was cold as ice.

She wanted ice. Her throat burned. From the smoke or from whatever cold she was catching now or from Andrew when he slammed her into the wall because she didn't give him the pipe back fast enough.

"My mother drives a Lexus."

"Not in here she doesn't. Put your hands behind your back. Don't make me tell you again."

"Or what? No honor roll this quarter? You can't do anything to me. I'm not even charged. I'm j'st waitin' to go home."

The look he gave her. Pure contempt. Like he was better than her.

"Your world's ending. You might try to get along in this one."

She looked away from him, up, not down. Took in the nowhere hallway they were in. Must be waiting for some idiot to open the next set of steel doors.

I've known plenty people been in here. We all get out.

But she hadn't been before. It was all new to Penny. New and scary and she didn't like being touched and she didn't like being told what to do. Her mother was an executive for a software company, worked in financials. Her father sent big checks every month to make up for never taking them up on those visitation rights. She had a scholarship for a Very Important School if that's where she chose to go.

I've known plenty people been in here. We all get out.

"Why do you talk like that?" Her mother had asked the other night at dinner. She was downing her fourth or fifth glass of Chablis. Her new boyfriend was sitting across the table in tennis shorts and a gold neck chain like some 90s reject.

"All my friends talk like this."

"You need new friends."

"Penelope Procolis?"

Damn, that door still echoed. She couldn't remember passing through the others. Still, she was here, some damn holding cell. She wondered where they'd taken everybody else.

Little Sierra town didn't have more than one Juvenile Justice Center. Hadn't seen Sif or Stev or – well, Andrew. He'd been going to The Big House.

Matron glared at her. Penny hadn't said anything, wasn't even really paying attention. Denial. Therapy me this: I'm not even here! Sweet smoke and she wouldn't be. Her throat hurt so bad, like she was still smoking. Might be able to cough some back up, get up on it all over again.

"Penelope Procolis? You *are* Penelope?"

"I'm Ms. Procolis," she said. Might as well let the woman know she wasn't going to be trifled with by someone who worked for the *state*. ...or was it the county?

Damn! Why'd she even give a shit?

"I said, you need to come with me."

"Where?"

The matron almost looked shocked, which was silly. Far more people must say "fuck you" than "where" and more must say "where" than "yes, ma'am, right away!"

Not being belligerent, though. She was just dizzy and getting really, really, really, really antsy. Wanted to GO. Wanted to DO SOMETHING.

Matron stopped glaring. Maybe the way Penny's hands kept throttling each other got to her. "Just the rest of intake, then a holding cell, then you'll see the judge."

Four o'clock Friday afternoon. She hadn't thought so.

"Is today Friday?"

Now the guard looked positively sympathetic. "Yes. Come on."

Damn those doors. Her head ached. They'd let her clean up. A little. Still bloody from the wreck. Damn Stev, if he was that messed up, he shouldn't've been driving.

Tell us. Hadn't they always said that? Tell us. Designated driver was always supposed to be the one seein' the least amount of white lines in the middle of the damn road.

Back through four out of five of the doors, back to where she'd almost started only now she faced a door marked Court. And for the first time, her stomach felt pre-smoke. All those worms.

"Butterflies!" her mother always said brightly when Penny was afraid before swimming lessons or ballet lessons or gymnastics lessons or martial arts lessons or those horrible French lessons with the guy who used to feel her up and then, as a result of that, she'd get nervous before therapy lessons.

Therapy lessons. Giggle.

But still afraid. "And they're not butterflies, Mummy. They're worms. Big ole maggots, eatin' out my belly."

"Why do you *talk* like that?"

"Why do you sleep with your tennis instructor?" That's cliché.

Even through the damn door, standing there, realizing they were going to wait right here until it was her turn, "So you might as well sit down."

Screw that, I'll pace, yeah, my hands are safely behind my back, you outweigh me by 100 pounds, you cow —

Even through that damn door, bang and crash of solid steel, she could hear the screaming.

From the courtroom.

"What *is* that?" First voluntary thing she'd said to any of them.

Wished she hadn't.

Guard smiled. Grim and satisfied. Like she'd just bitten the head off something she planned to eat that wasn't quite dead yet.

"Sentencing."

Penny stood on her tiptoes and peered through the tiny,

steel-webbed crack of glass. "For *what?*"

But the guard just said, "Sit down."

First really bad bit of luck: the judge was a woman. Middle aged, blond hair out of a bottle. Lipstick on crooked. The big blue eyes and real blond hair thing worked much better on men. Never been in court before, but she'd have given odds it'd work there, too.

Didn't work so much on women, unless they were a little funny, and even then, she was a minor. Funny didn't usually lapse over into hilarious, especially with court officials, she'd guess, and those who wanted to keep their jobs. Even if they were that way, Penny set them off – too slim, too pretty, too young, too smart. Who'd not be jealous?

First offense, though.

Yeah, right. First time caught. Saw that in the judge's eyes, too, but she was busy doing Therapy Face – concerned, contrite, convincing.

But that door. That finality sound. That SLAM. That thunk. Slamthunk. Gods, she couldn't figure how to say it. That 'End Of The World' sound.

And all the screaming, too. The screaming that had come right through the doors. Almost enough to make her straight. Sober.

Judge did, too. Serious. Straighten up. Stop thinking about Andrew's dreds and Stev's fucked up driving and Mom's tennis pro.

"What do you have to say for yourself?"

She wasn't sure what the judge had actually said. That wasn't it. But it was something. Some request for information or explanation or rationalization. Penny covered her confusion in a very convincing coughing fit that became real when some of the smoke lodged in her throat.

Gods, how much was still left in her? Was she on fire? Were her lungs on fire? Damn, had Andrew given her something other than smoke? Damn, damn, had Andrew given her something other than a cold?

Wait. Someone had asked her something.

She finished coughing. "Could you repeat the question?" Staring winsomely at the judge.

The judge rolled her eyes. It was the clerk, anyway. "State your name," he said, like she was an idiot.

"Oh."

He tiny, bespectacled clerk leaned very close to his machine and entered her name, poking each key with a quill.

First offense. Blond eyed, blue haired. Um. First offense. Honor roll, student council, yearbook staff, French club. No demerits on her driver's license. Only sixteen years old. Straight shot at ivy league if no city or state or county level drone bottle blond bitch screwed it up. *So come the hell on and let me walk.*

Because that's what happens in these cases, right?

The Latino girl who'd been glaring at her in lockdown. She'd get Juvenile Justice. She'd get detention.

The other girl, swarthy and wasn't that a good word? Swwwwarthy. The girl who'd been barfing. She'd get detention. Lockdown. Lockup.

Andrew. Those dreds. Yeah, baby. Stateside.

But blond and blue and true?

My mother drives a Lexus.

What had all that screaming been? Didn't the guard say Sentencing? But she's just trying to trip you.

When she looked around the courtroom again the judge was triplicate. Penny shook her head in disgust. Freakin' smoke.

But they weren't identical. Wasn't that TV-out-of-focus smoke blur. There were three bottle blond judges, each a tiny bit different than the last, and damned if she looked middle aged anymore, more like mummies in the antiquities exhibit last year.

She thought one of them was knitting.

Girl, you are freakin'.

Then here came the questions.

"Do you know what you're doing to yourself?"

"Do you understand how dangerous those drugs are?"

"Have you tried therapy for your addictions?"

"How many times have you smoked it?" (And shouldn't she've asked that before the addiction question?)

"How are your grades? School activities?"

"Parents divorced. How are you handling that?"

She answered, wide eyed and knock kneed. She should've been in a Catholic school girl uniform. Innocent blond girl.

She did know what she was doing, but it had only been once. Maybe twice. It was peer pressure, your honor, and never mind those people were not at all her peers, Stev, maybe, and Jolie, but Andrew was your basic knockoff, the kind she'd never have again. She'd marry and breed with someone polite who asked before he kissed her too hard whereas Andrew would back her into a wall and –

Therapy, yes. It was quite helpful at the time, ma'am. Grades are straight A's. Honor roll, student government, yearbook.

Parents? *I don't have parents, I have mannequins. Wind up toys.* But she said something out of the Book of Answers. Something Approved.

Judge firmed her lips. she looked at the file in front of her. she looked at what she was knitting, which was short and blood red and looked finished somehow even though the yarn still held it to the ball.

Judge turned to confer with the judges on either side of her. Penny blinked very hard several times, trying to dispel the illusion. There were *not* triplets on the bench.

One blond judge leaned way, way, way over the very high bench and stared at Penny as if she couldn't make her out any better than Penny could make her out. The other just kept shaking her head and when the one in the middle tried to argue with her, she smacked her hand down on the desk and leaned over the middle judge's knitting, gave Penny a look of pure malice, and snipped the yarn at the ball.

"She's been courting Death. Let Death court her."

The knitting fell away.

The three judges turned as one and stared at Penny.

"Guilty."

"This isn't a trial, it's a hearing!" Penny protested. "Arraignment." Her father, Mr. Big Checks Invisible Man, was a lawyer.

"Guilty."

"No, you can't, I'm going to Princeton, I – "

"Guilty!" the third judge yelled.

"Sentence," the clerk said. His little round eyeglasses reflected light so he looked like he had no eyes.

"I haven't seen my mother!" Penny screamed. "has she even been told? I haven't seen a lawyer. My daddy's a lawyer. You can't do this!"

"Sentence," the clerk said again, as if the mummies might forget.

"Death!" roared the judges

Penny screamed. *Andy, what did you give me? Andy, what did you give me? Andy, what the hell did you give me, I can't wake up. I can't wake UP.*

She turned to run. Had to be some way out. Everyone else got in and out.

I known plenty of people been in here. We all get out.

Get out, get out, get out.

She got all the way to the door, heart beating wildly on a combination of toxic adrenaline and pure terror and a bit of smoke still slowing her down when they caught her.

Guards. Twins, maybe. What was it with this place and multiples? Two big, big guys, like Andrew's contact big, and they were not smiling and they were not offering a good time. One on each elbow, they lifted her up off the floor, cute little blue eyed blond haired thing, always prided herself on being tiny. Mummy had always said skinny was better.

The smoke made that so much easier but now she'd trade everything to be a cow like that guard and be able to break free.

They dumped her back in front of the judge. One judge again. She was way too fucked up for this. Maybe they hadn't said what she though they said. What she thought *she'd* said, one judge.

She shook her head to clear it.

The judge was looking at her. "Oh, yes," she said, as if the clearing head shake had been meant for her. And then, to the guards, "Why did you bring her here? Carry out the sentence."

She didn't even bother to look at Penny again.

"Nonononononononono – "

Probably just bound over for trial, that would sound like a death sentence to anyone with a future like hers waiting. Her father was going to be pissed and Mummy wouldn't be any too pleased.

But that's all it was. She'd imagined the rest.

"It's not what you think, it's not what you think, it's not what you think."

"Yes, it is," the guards said, and carried her through another huge steel-core door.

Slam.

The sound of it would echo in her head hours later.

Her head was *really* aching.

"Where are we going?"

No response. She wasn't really going anywhere, more being carried, which meant, okay fine, she was going, but not willingly. Not of her own volition.

They don't kill first offense honor students who use the word volition. Get *straight*.

She looked from one to the other of the guards. Enormous, muscled, almost good looking if they weren't too old and not really on her side and – what was she thinking? "Please," Penny said. "Please tell me where we're going?"

The guards' eyes met over her head. They set her on the hard tile and allowed her to walk between them.

"You were sentenced," one of them said.

"We're taking you to carry out the sentence."

She felt dizzy. Like she might faint. Almost wished they'd carry her again because her legs were too heavy. Only she didn't want to go at all, so she wished they'd let her stop and rest so she wouldn't be so dizzy and confused.

"I haven't even had a trial yet. I haven't even had an *attorney* yet," she said reasonably, looking from one to the other. Neither looked at her, just at each other and straight forward again.

The hall smelled like orange Starburst candy, or pine scented cleaner, or old cafeteria food. They were moving through sections of Juvenile Justice at a good pace.

"You were tried, convicted, sentenced, decreed," one of the guards said.

"We're taking you to carry out the sentence."

"But – "

Steel door number five. Just a holding cell. Take a deep breath.

Steel door number six. Okay, maybe it's farther in.

They walked for what seemed like days. Penny drifted in and out. Amorphous, like her thoughts. Sometimes when the guards tried to hold her elbows they held each other's hands instead. Then they'd look confused and grab each other again and then they'd make the effort and grab her.

When the smoke surged inside her she'd swirl faster and faster, along the ceiling, along the walls, moving at the speed of light, but the guards were always right there at her elbows. Supporting her. Helpful creatures, the guards. Further they moved through the Juvenile Justice Center, the less human they looked. Penny didn't really like that.

Steel door number thirty-five.

Steel door number thirty-six.

They're not taking you to a holding cell, sweetie.

"Is it getting darker?"

They looked at each other over her head again, then looked at her for a change. Why did everybody keep looking at her like she was an idiot?

"Well, of course it's getting darker. For you."

"For you."

She didn't like that answer, so she didn't ask anything else.

She thought about Andrew, instead, and what she'd say to him when she saw him again, because this was *not* the usual stuff, this was something laced with something mixed with something else and she did *not* like it.

"Stop."

They'd been walking for hours. She was glad to stop. Her feet felt like they were bleeding.

"This is where you're going."

"What?"

Gods. Whatever he'd given her had really messed her up. They stood at a T junction of halls. She could still smell old cafeteria grease and cleaning fluids and the weird orange candy smell and stale teenage boy smell but over all of it, she smelled something wet. Like wet dirt.

Right in front of her, where the hall should be. A river.

Right.

But there *was* a river there. And it was darker her, way darker than it had been in the building and even if it were five o'clock now, six o'clock, it didn't make sense to be so dark. It was only mid-September, still light out till late. And the building had electricity, didn't it?

But then, there was this river. And it spanned like a double hallway's width. And past that she couldn't really make out what she saw. Looked like a cave, or something and – let's not be silly.

She leaned past the walls of the hall that she stood in, the hall that butted up to the river, leaned carefully out and stared in both directions. Just river, running to what she assumed was north, dark water, blackness all around. She turned back and stared at the guards, who stood unperturbed, waiting for something. Penny turned back and peered along the river in the other direction.

There was something there. Something moving toward her out of the darkness. Something bone white, dead bone white, like the maggots she'd said were crawling in her stomach, said it just to irritate her mother.

She wanted her mother. She did not want whatever was coming toward her up this river.

"What?" she said. She wanted to say, "What is that?" but fear caught in her throat.

The guards did not look at all human now. She couldn't say what she thought they were. They caught her elbows and turned her back toward them. Her eyes moved back and forth between them, and she was talking nonstop, asking them questions, trying to get past them.

One guard took her head in his hands. The other took her feet. They picked her up as if she were a board and Penny tried to thrash, tried to scream, indignation mixed with frantic terror mixed with *I've got to get out of here* and all they did was lay her down, flat on her back.

No, not rape, this isn't happening, not now, not here, not – not rape. One of them closed her eyes. One of them opened her mouth. She felt something cold and metal against her closed eyes. She tasted something metal and dirty against her tongue.

She heard the boat brush up against the shore.

The ferryman wore a cloak. Under it he seemed to have no face. He took the coins from her eyes and mouth and pulled her into the boat and Penny was afraid to argue with him.

He has no face.

That was crazy. It was just hidden under his cloak, that's all. Shadowy, here. Dark. The boat rocked on the river she refused to believe in, a dark black river that wound slowly down through the Juvenile Justice Center and she could still see things around her, holding cells and dorm cells and an exercise room and even a classroom where everybody was reading something. A few of the kids looked up as she went by. One of the girls made a kissing face at her and winked.

"Where are you taking me?"

The bone boat dipped and swayed on the water. Inside Penny the smoke dipped and swayed. Sick and scared and angry now. What were her parents *thinking*? Was this some kind of intervention?

I don't need anything like that, I'm fine, I know what I'm doing. I'm Scholarship Girl. I'll show them. For doing this. I'll show them.

She hadn't figured out how yet when the boat bumped to the shore again, this time across what would have been the hall if they were still in the Justice Center, but somewhere along the river they'd left that behind. They came out into a gray meadow, fields of gray and black and white grasses blowing in a wind she could neither see nor feel, a cavernous sky overhead, something distant and yet confining, a sky and yet a ceiling. Something circled there, something huge with leathery wings.

"Where are we?" she asked the ferryman.

"Get out of the boat," he said. His voice scratched like tree limbs.

"But where are we?" She wasn't getting out until somebody told her something.

The ferryman turned his eyeless face toward her. He did have a face, after all, sallow and pinched and dried to a husk. Blinded, eyeless. Merciless.

"You're home," he said. "Get out of the boat."

She gripped the sides of it, her knuckles white as the bone boat. "Take me back. I demand you take me back. They can't do this to me." Whatever this was. "You can't do this. Take me back."

"You have paid the fare," he said. The coins from her eyes and mouth clinked in the bag he held up. "You cannot return. Get out of the boat."

And she was out, on the bank of the black river, the boat

moving away from her back toward the light. Penny raged after him. Coming down hard. Reality setting in *here* where she couldn't do anything about it, here where she was lost.

"Come back. Come back. Please, please, come back."

Up river, then. Just like a nature hike. A freakin' hike. That's what she needed. Wanted. Whatever this was, intervention, hallucination, whatever it was, someone was going to get their ass kicked for it.

"This is not acceptable!" she shrieked. She sounded like her mother. Soon, she'd be sleeping with tennis pros. She resolved not to yell anymore. Just walk out. Way in had to be the way out.

Oily black river water. Black dirt. Glints of light came from the cavern ceiling, which hemmed her in and yet was too far away to see. There and not there. Fever dream. Smoke dream.

"This isn't happening, you know," Penny said.

Black flowers in the black dirt. Impossible. High school biology said there could never be black flowers or even blue roses. Even her mother, who could grow *anything*. Even *she* couldn't grow black or blue. Something about pigmentation or photosynthesis or – or something. "There are no black flowers," she said.

The man holding the spray of black roses knelt on one knee in front of her, blocking her path back. He held them out to her, and laughed when she jolted back so hard and fast she almost unbalanced into the thick, sluggish river.

"Nothing happens here," he said. "It' can't. but to the extent that it can, it is, and you are here, at last."

She stared at him, aghast.

Black hair, black eyes, black beard and if he stood up, what, fifteen feet tall?

"My queen," he said.

II. Clotho (The Present)

Denny parked the Lexus in the most remote corner she could find. This was *not* a place to bring a car like this, parked in a Public Parking lot beside a lot of Hyundai and other tin cans. Shouldn't be here at all, her or the car. Someone had most certainly screwed up.

No way in hell Penelope should be here, not with Brad's influence, for god's sake. He was her father, and a very important man, a very important *partner* in the firm and the judge just had her clerk tell him to get his ass down to the Juvenile Justice Center if he wanted to know what was going on with Penny, just like everyone else had to do when they wanted to know what was going on with their kids.

We're not everyone else, Denny thought. *This is ridiculous. Penelope is an honor student. Who the hell arrests an honor student?*

She locked the door, set the alarm, and only just caught herself from tumbling over into the car. Big blast of wind, something arctic and way too early for mid-September. Denny blinked several times fast and stared around the parking lot.

Dust and dirt and discarded papers were starting to swirl in ever expanding eddies, floating head level and up. The wind caught her skirt, and felt like ice against her skin.

Some kind of early storm? Great. Just what we needed. Her high heels smacked the concrete smartly. She clicked toward the entrance and all the time she was wondering what idiot had decided to arrest her daughter, arrest *Penelope*, it was absurd, even if she was letting off some steam –

I told her, I told her to stop doing that stuff, I told her it was stupid, it would make her stupid, she's stupid, she has to get into Princeton, silly little bitch –

--still, there's such a thing as common courtesy. We live in The Mount, for god's sake. You don't just arrest kids from The Mount.

The wind battered her, as if trying to drive her into the building. Denny kept herself straight and upright, every muscle tight against it. Damn wind felt like it was coming right out of the dead of winter. Had to have dropped 30 degrees in the last 10 minutes.

What the hell? Around her a few other people were running in and out of the building, shivering in the sudden chill.

She blew through the door, stopped inside to catch her breath and straighten her hair and renew her righteous indignation. You do not just arrest kids from The Mount. You do *not*.

Apparently they did, though. And Denise Procolis had to follow the signs and directions and ask the receptionist where she needed to go. Her high heels made sharp, punishing sounds on the linoleum and her suit felt too warm now that she was inside.

"I'm looking for my daughter. Penelope Procolis."

"Take a number. Take a seat. We'll call you."

The storm had moved inside of her. For an instant, Denny couldn't breathe. She gripped the edge of the Intake Reception cubicle until the words could come out in normal sentences again and at levels that humans, not just dogs, could hear.

"I said, I'm looking for my daughter."

"And *I* said, take a number, take a seat." The girl behind the counter was either very pregnant or very fat. What she wasn't was very impressed with Denise Procolis. She looked up finally, pointed at the red cartel of numbers much like ice cream shops had, and went back to whatever she was doing on her computer.

How *dare* they?

Her number was 76. They were currently talking to number 57. Denise fumed briefly, looked around, saw a woman missing two teeth and needing work on several others, assumed (correctly) that she was also waiting for a chance to talk about her child, assumed again that the woman would rather have an extra $50 than see her child 20 minutes sooner, and assumed one more time that she could probably make the same transaction for $25, and did so.

The officer of the court wore red. A knitted red something that Denise couldn't make out. The judge looked – blurry.

Denise was getting a bad taste in her mouth. She was starting to remember something she didn't want to remember. She was starting to understand the storm outside, and to understand herself.

I left all this behind.

She hadn't.

We live on The Mount. You can't do this to us.

They had.

She sat down across from the judge, tried one more time to make the red thing around her neck make sense, and said, "I'm here about my daughter, Penelope Procolis. I hear you have her here." She folded her hands across her purse in her lap and wished that women still wore gloves. Somehow, holding a pair of gloves in one hand would seem even more formal, professional.

"We did have her here," the judge said. She was studying a file intently and frowning, as if reminding herself of something that had happened long ago.

"It was just a couple *hours* ago," Denny said.

"we did have her here a couple hours ago," the judge said brightly, as if pleased they were in agreement. "Don't have her here any more." Pursed her lips, shook her head. Was that it? Was she finished?

Denise breathed in through her nose. "Where is she?"

The judge brightened. "Oh. Oh, yes." She smiled. "Tried. Sentenced. Decreed. Executed."

Denny felt the room sliding toward her and grabbed the sides of the chair to keep her balance. "She's *dead*?"

The judge frowned, obviously replaying her words. Laughed. "No, no, the *decree* was executed. The *sentence* was carried out."

Denise took a deep breath. "Atropus, what have you done with my daughter?"

The judge smiled. No doubt her sisters were here, nearby. They traveled together, but Denny recognized her now.

"The thread is not cut," she said. "She is in the underworld. She is home. She is with her future husband."

Denny closed her eyes. I drive a Lexus. My daughter is an honor student. We live on *The Mount*.

"My daughter is with Hades?" But it was more of a statement.

"Fate," Atropus said, and laughed. "We are the law."

"We'll see," Denny said.

She tried calling Bard from the lobby of the Justice Center but couldn't get any reception. Her phone cycled through networks and the helpful pregnant-or-fat receptionist called out to her that almost no one ever got through, they all had to go outside.

"It's all the steel in this place," she said helpfully.

That's probably part of it, Denny thought.

Outside the parking lot was a white-out. A blizzard raged through what had been a pleasant late summer September afternoon. Wind drove her skirt into her legs and pinned it so she could barely walk. Snow found its way through her blouse and into her eyes and in the toes of her sling backs.

Snow, winter, grief.

Her car door was frozen shut. She beat on it with one fist, pointless and insignificant, went around to the passenger side where the wind hadn't blown the snow into the lock and climbed in. She tried calling Brad but his secretary told her he was in depositions and would likely be there for the next week and a half, nonstop. That this didn't seem at all odd to the girl on the phone just meant that things were playing out the way they wanted to and not the way Denny wanted them to. She thanked the little twit and hung up.

Fine. Atropus wouldn't be any help.

But some of her minions would.

I'm not dressed for this, she thought. *Donna Karen?* And it was cold. *Damn it, Penelope.*

She went back to reception, back past the pregnant blond who called after her and told her she couldn't get through and anyway someone had to buzz her. They were steel core doors and they made a hideous sound when they banged around her. Denny put her hand on the first one and squinted through Estee Lauder until the vines came up from the dirt under the hideous, filthy, pine-scented floor and choked their way through the tumblers and locks.

The guards met her after she got through the fifth door. "Visitors must sign in. Visiting hours are Wednesday and Saturday between three o'clock and six o'clock in the afternoon. This is a lockdown facility."

This was not her forte. Mostly she just grew things. Created nice little butterflies, like the kind people felt in their stomachs before something exciting happened. Not maggots, like Penelope insisted on saying she felt in her stomach. Not maggots like these two standing here, between her and her daughter. But she'd learned a lot living on The Mount. She'd learned a lot on her way to becoming World President of the Financial Division of a Major Software Company.

"Take me to her," she said in the voice of the storm outside and the few natural fibers in the guards' shirts writhed into frenetic life and began swarming over their faces, around their necks, down their throats.

They got her there rather more swiftly than they'd taken Penny. Denny looked at the black river and groaned. Knowing what she was going to find wasn't the same as seeing it.

"Just please, please, Penelope, don't have taken anything."

The guards grinned at her. Denny thought about the storm outside, the ice and the fabric from their shirts, tightened her fist and froze the strands around the men's necks.

The guards stopped grinning and froze, hands tugging the fabric away from their throats. Denny turned back to the river. Black, oily, foul water. No sign of the ferryman, of course, but then he wouldn't be here for her.

Fine. She drew three gold pieces from her bag, more than required but sufficient enough to invoke interest even in the most reticent. She threw the coins into the water. "Charon!"

The bone boat looked a lot like a yellow cab. The ferryman wore a jaunty cap over his jaundiced, paper dry flesh. Denny sighed. "Take me to my daughter," she said. It wasn't like they hadn't gone through this, one way or the other, before.

Penelope, just for once in your life, say no.

Penny said yes. Yes, yes, yes. Gods, here she was, millions of miles from home, dead some said, and now she's supposed to marry this guy. *Marry* him, and sure, he was good looking, buff and all, but he had to be at least her mother's age, and how gross was that? So when it turned out he was holding, she said yes.

He was weird, anyway. Kept talking about her being the springtime and her place was here and the natural order would change. Called her Core or something, first she'd thought he'd said 'whore' and she'd had quite enough of being called that by Andrew, thankyouverymuch. Called her the Maiden, too, which she thought was just messed up.

And they were underground. In some kind of enormous cave. It gave her the willies to think about it. Fields stretched out as far as she could see, all gray and haunted and dead, and there were people everywhere, every-frickin-where and they were just kind of *there*, lost and wandering around and moaning and when the guy who she was supposed to marry said, "This, all this, will be yours," she gagged and wanted to run.

But he had drugs. More than even Andrew could go through. Piles of pills, stashes of rocks and pipes and fix kits and you name it. A lot of it she'd never seen before and a lot of it she didn't understand, but he said he'd explain it to her.

"Just tell me what it is you want the most," he said and she thought again that he seemed gentle, but somehow – *inexorable*, and she should get extra credit for that word. There was something about him, something that made her feel no matter what she wanted, eventually he'd get what *he* waned. That he was patient. Like a spider, waiting to trap something in its web. It made her feel uncomfortable, that maggoty feeling in her belly again, and she wanted her mother and she wanted to go home and she wanted to be high again, and mostly, most of all –

"I want not to feel," she said.

It was a pile of light blue pills. They tasted something like chalk, or overripe raspberries. They tasted of sleep and forgetting.

She took four of them before the world went away and stopped bothering her.

"She's been courting Death. Let Death court her," the judges said.

"You are my Queen," Hades said.

"Just, please, Penelope, for once in your life, say no," Denny said.

III. Atropus (The Future)

Penny held a handful of blue pills. This was what had gotten her into this. Maybe it could get her back out. Or at least restore some kind of balance.

The Maiden slept. The Mother came looking. The Crone held the thread between Life and Death.

The world above, locked in snow, locked in winter, slept.

A bit autobiographical this one, because if I could have stopped the exact same "lifestyle center" from ruining a beautiful chunk of Reno, I would have. And if I'd thought of Jenna's line about strip malls, I would have used it. Unfortunately, the line was thought up by my husband when I ranted at him about the interview with the developer.

This one is for the coyote I saw at the base of Mt Rose one beautiful frosted Christmas morning.

City Limits

Moonlight glinted off structural steel, points of light forming new constellations. Skeletal steel arms stretched raw and heavy up toward vast and lightless Nevada skies. Even on the perimeter the city lights blocked the stars, dropped them to nothing more than light reflected off industrial foundations of the new mall.

Mt. Rose Highway. State Route 431. Head east and the road passes through sage and pinion and wild horses, up rock-strewn asphalt through hair-pin turns to Virginia City, home of the Comstock Lode and the Territorial Enterprise, where Mark Twain lived and wrote. A place where every summer camels still race, a preserved mining town hot and heavy with the smell of sage and the sleepy drone of crickets, where once, heading back down into Reno, Jenna had nearly driven off the road when an eagle lifted up from the abyss beyond the highway, gliding up on thermals, improbable as a dinosaur.

Head west, up Mt Rose Highway, off the curving freeway exit onto the State Route, and the road runs past the vacant sage and pine lot at the junction where last winter Jenna saw a coyote jogging over frozen ground on a mist-cold Christmas morning as she and Ted drove out to his folks' in Washoe Valley. Head west from that expanse of emptiness and there's Tahoe, pristine mountain lake known worldwide.

Home now of the raw, new, concrete and steel, piped-Muzak and Lexus-parking mall.

Lifestyle center. Not a mall. Mall was prosaic, old-fashioned. Not trendy enough. Not, maybe, rich enough for the trade expected here on the east side of the Sierra. Tourists in Reno no longer had the dread two hour trek over the mountain to the Mecca of Sacramento to shop; discretionary income could stay in Reno, Biggest Little City in the World, such a great Lifestyle, Quality of Life, beautiful place to live with air quality and affordable housing and employment opportunities, come one, come all. Come California. And it did. They did.

Jenna turned off the tired Honda, which gave a whimper and shuddered. There wasn't much to see yet. Just steel, plunging upwards, foundations like slabs of city washed up in an inland sea, structural steel like a sketchy outline of the buildings that would follow. A Dillard's, whatever that was. Pottery Barn. Another Home Depot, surely there weren't enough yet to walk the entire city by going from Home Depot to Home Depot. All of it upscale. All of it concrete and asphalt and that many more cars that much closer to Tahoe. More traffic, more pollution, more people, more trash. Landscaped with grass, not natural to the area, the sage and juniper ripped out because of people's allergies.

Because they weren't pretty enough once the concrete and asphalt and retail came.

She let her head drop back and stared up at the sky, but the stars weren't visible out here any longer.

A hot rush of anger filled her. Anger and pain at all the losses. At squirrels and rabbits, coyotes and scrub jays, meadow larks and crows forced out, natural growth gone, dirt covered over so the city could expand and the people who could afford it could shop and the city could petition for a Nordstrom's.

She hated the sick, twisting powerlessness, hated knowing tomorrow she'd drop back into Jenna Freelance Writer, writing a business article on Retail in Nevada and interviewing Mr. Foothills Lifestyle Center developer who was already back in Georgia planning assaults on other innocent communities across the country. No one would listen. Even if they felt the loss of beauty and the essentials of Nevada, the good of the shoppers outweighed the good of those who just wanted to see empty space and preferred the sound of wind off Mt Rose to the sound of muzak, preferred the scent of sage to the smell of economy-boosting discretionary income.

"*Damn it.*" Her fists balled. She was out here alone in the night. Ted expected her home from critique group soon, but not yet, and this was foolish. "I don't <u>care</u>." She bent, picked up a rock, hurled it and missed everything and that made her even angrier. She shouted and threw handfuls of rocks, tiny useless sounds against the steel supports as she raged into the desert-scented night: "Go HOME. We don't need you here. Go home, go home, go *home*. Stop hurting us!"

Sharp pain against her calf brought her out of it. She'd run forward, stumbling, shouting incoherent threats to nameless, ever-blameless corporations, there was never *anyone* to blame, economic authorities just did their jobs, developers developed what the people wanted, what, at least, they said the people wanted, and no one listened to animals, no one cared about the sound of the wind or the smells of a summer night.

She'd run up against a stab of Rebar poking up out of the fresh asphalt, bent at just the right angle to cut her leg open. Moonlight lit the blood on her skin, through weave of sandal, down across the tar and asphalt, thin red line dripping down onto the dirt past the Rebar. Jenna stared, as if something had changed.

When she stood up, they were there. Three figures stood on the unnatural ridge of hillside torn out of the earth by the creation of the parking lot. Tall against the background of trees, three figures, one woman, two men, and Jenna should leave, go home before she found out they were South Reno 13, who liked to tag dead smack in the center of Reno, which meant either they had no sense of direction or that they were expanding their territory, she didn't need to know which and Ted was going to kill her if he found out about this, it was *stupid*, being out here—

But there was no menace. No feeling of harm from the three who stood against the moonlight. Next instant, they were gone.

The Honda started without protest. The drive home was quiet. The air smelled like sage.

"How was critique group?" Ted's attention came and went in three or four minute intervals. He muted commercials, watched local news with rapt attention. "What'd they think of the story?"

Jenna shrugged. "Metaphor."

Ted grinned at her. "You told me that before you left. Could've stayed here and had glorious spaghetti with me."

Jenna made a face. "I've had your spaghetti and glorious is definitely giving it spin."

Ted remained un-phased. "If you'd stayed, you could have made something other than spaghetti. Which story was it?"

On the TV, happy peppy people danced about low fat fast food, living fantasy lives. Jenna dragged her eyes away from the spectacle. "The one about the desert, and the new mall."

The dislike in her voice was thick and flat, but she'd gotten Ted's full attention. He grinned. "I think we've got that account," he said as if it was something she'd been waiting to hear. He waited for her delight.

Jenna shut her mouth and stared at him. He knew how she felt about Progress with a capital P, progress that advanced nothing but greed. It just didn't seem to *matter* to him. As if he thought it was all an act on her part. Or as if of course she'd change her beliefs when it came to him.

I wish I could, she thought. She wanted to believe someone understood. She wanted to believe she was close to someone, that somewhere she fit.

Ted snuggled close, murmured something incoherent that sounded like *banana cake*, and fell asleep, arms around her. Jenna stared out the bedroom window at the old apple tree picked out in moonlight while the evening's events played behind her eyes, muddling themselves together as sleep edged nearer, until she sat with the other writers from her critique group in plastic chairs at metal tables on the steel and concrete piers of the new mall and the desert washed up around them in waves, dirt and stones and scratchy sage washing up to their feet and away again.

"The premise is interesting, but it's only a literary device, one's own power of mind effecting change," Diane said, but Diane hated fantasy and hated that Jenna sold so much of it.

"I like the construct of the mall as enemy," Sydney said. "But of course you're just resistant to change and it doesn't work as story."

"I think you are lecturing," one of the editors of a major science fiction magazine said, and she had to be dreaming, there were no editors in critique group. "It's a polemic, not a story, and it just didn't grab me, alas."

Jenna stared at them. They were hard to see because the night was so dark and all the stars had gone out.

"I think you should stop this one and write something else," they all said together and now somehow they all looked exactly like the developer of the Foothills Lifestyle Center — *you've never even seen him* — and they stood, threatening, but Jenna looked past them at the hillside and suddenly they were inconsequential.

Three beings stood on the artificial berm, limned in moonlight, right as everything else was wrong.

One female, two males. One summer-brown cottontail, one coyote, one crow. Desert creatures. She waited for the big horn sheep, but it didn't come.

They ran late the next morning, which was normal. Woke after both alarms with no memory of hearing either. Which was also normal. Ted went off to another day in PR land and Jenna went running through their old tree-shaded neighborhood and then over-caffeinated in an attempt to be ready for her phone interview with the developer.

The developer and <u>his</u> PR person.

"Why do PR people do conference calls with writers?"

she asked Ted repeatedly and he'd give her a different answer every time. *Because we don't trust writers. Because we don't trust media. Because we don't trust the CEO.*

It seemed to come down to a lack of trust.

This PR person whispered answers to Jenna's questions and the developer parroted them back: about local contractors and subs, which made the developer tangent away into how lifestyle centers employed people in downtrodden, retail-insufficient towns. Jenna, who thought that malls needed employees anyway, found this an insufficient example of community involvement and asked for more. The developer said he'd get specifics and Jenna heard the PR person panicking and turning pages rapidly, looking for documentation of good deeds.

Uh huh, she thought.

Jenna had questions from her editor for the article: acreage, square-footages, anchor stores, projected economic impact. Why the developer saw fit to pick on Reno, though phrased as what made Reno a target market, emphasis on *target*.

The developer didn't want to answer questions. He wanted to complain. That Reno was under-served in retail opportunities, which Jenna privately thought should make him happy. That there wasn't enough land for retail opportunities within the city. When Jenna asked what was occupying the land it turned out to be other retail that had already been opportunistic. When she pointed out that maybe they weren't under-served, then, the developer changed the subject. He complained that labor was hard to find (because in the wake of the housing boom, everyone was now building retail, Jenna pointed out, and the PR guy whispered and the developer charged on angrily.)

He complained that landscaping was a nightmare, that it

was impossible to find water here for all their grass. Jenna choked on startled laughter and said it was, after all, a <u>desert</u>.

The developer asked what else she needed to know.

Why us?

Jenna asked for a description of the lifestyle center and was suddenly drowning in talk about how 700 acres would have piped Muzak, outdoor dining, grass, flowers, trees, drive-up access to stores.

"Drive up access?"

"All the stores are approached from the exterior," the developer said. "It's all outdoors, actually, campus style buildings."

Jenna thought for an instant, bit her tongue, and said it anyway. "So it's a strip mall?"

For an instant the developer only sputtered, then, "You listen to me," he said but the line seemed to go dead and abruptly the PR guy was there, no whispering but loud and upset, something about Foothills Lifestyle Center and Reno and she thought she heard things she couldn't have before the line went dead again but just before she said "Hello?" the developer said out of the dead line, "What have you <u>done</u>?" and the phone slammed down.

"Testy," Jenna said, but already the pull was on her, like a sickness, something dragging her from her desk, she had her keys, her notebook, her purse, hurry, just hurry, just <u>hurry</u>.

The freeway entrance was blocked off. Detour signs directed her down Kietzke Lane where she did not want to go. Jenna turned onto Vassar and came to a complete stop just before the old staid post office.

July sun simmered off midmorning asphalt and all the cars piled up together where drivers had abandoned them. Jenna stalled the Honda, cut the motor and stepped onto the burning asphalt to gape with the crowd.

Across from the post office the federal administration building had recently grown up, cutting down 50 year old trees, scrub grass, rubble, squirrels, birds and the occasional urban raccoon. Only now it was gone again, a rubble of glass and framing supports, flat as if a bomb had hit it. The woman next to Jenna kept saying "Terrorist attack" into her cell phone but Jenna didn't think so. The building looked as if it had been – shoved up, off the earth, not exploded down into it.

She watched a blue belly lizard crawl up out of the wreckage and stand puffing its sides, purple in the emergency lights. No one around her saw it, or cared. Voices filled the morning air, the sun simmered. Sirens wailed, drew closer, others continued past. The police roped off the scene, the falling building and the rubble and the lizard– and the green.

She ducked her head to see past the crowd, past the cop who spread his arms, shooing everyone back as if they were geese or chickens. There was green, growing up out of the falling building, like sage or the tops of trees, and beside the leaves and branches, a human arm poked up, waving feebly.

Jenna spun, hands to mouth, stomach heaving. All around her people exclaimed and pressed forward, pushing closer as Jenna struggled to get past them and out. Away.

Of course there were people in there, what did you think?

The Honda started and there was a hole in the traffic around it, enough room to get out of the snarl of cars and back on the street.

Ted didn't answer his cell, it just rang over to voice mail. Jenna tossed her own phone in the passenger's seat, and drove, fast, toward the new mall, the <u>hurry</u> still dragging her, the panic she'd heard in the developer's voice.

Everywhere at the crossroads steel had fallen, concrete cracked. Jenna abandoned the Honda half a mile up Mt Rose at an old grocery-anchored shopping center and even then getting close meant getting past sheriff's deputies and flashing lights.

Her progress was sure-footed. She was as confident moving across the sage and scree-covered hillside outside the mall as other people were helpless and flailing. She was in her element, same as she ever was in the desert, without others.

Midday summer sun colored everything flat hot white, unreal and overexposed. Jenna slipped between the crowd and headed for shouting whenever she heard it, using altercations to pass distracted sheriffs. She dodged past hands struck out to catch and stop her and wriggled free of someone who actually caught the back of her t-shirt. The air was full of voices, reporters swearing, cameramen muttering about feeds, small voices she couldn't make out but for their jubilance and celebration.

Closer and closer, she saw only people, no mall, only the shifting crowd and flashing lights.

Because there was no mall.

It was gone.

Vertigo hit her, so hard she stumbled, one hand out for balance but there was nothing and no one to grab and she fell to one knee, sickness vomiting up inside her at what she couldn't be seeing.

Crossroads. Two hundred acres of sage and pinion where she'd seen the coyote on Christmas morning.

Jenna gagged. Nobody came near her. Over the roaring in her ears she could hear the crackle of police radios, people screaming into cell phones, reporters arguing.

And the voices again, clearer, and closer.

Where the concrete and steel had been, the ground grew up, unnatural as the carved-out hillside had been, as if overnight the desert had come in and raised the foundation. Reclaimed– itself. Destroyed and covered over the intruder as the mall had overcome the desert.

"Are you all right?" someone asked.

Jenna nodded but couldn't look away. Someone helped her to her feet. "What do you think?" the man asked.

"I don't know." Her voice sounded dry as the desert. Ancient.

Voices. *We're here.*

"What?"

He hadn't spoken, looked at her strangely. "Bulldozers, maybe?"

She nodded. "Must be." Impossible. That would leave tracks. She wanted him to move away, be quiet. *Let me think.*

"I just don't see how they did it," he said to someone else.

What have you done? The snarl in the developer's voice, she couldn't remember his name, suddenly, just The Developer, had to have it in her notes, didn't she? "What have you done?"

"Who are you?" someone behind her asked. "Are you press? Because I can tell you everything, I saw it all–"

"No, excuse me, I'm not, I have to go–" She pressed back through the crowd that parted around her like tide. Like sage in the wind. Voices, press, police, people. *We are here. We've come.* Joyous voices, like something good had happened.

Before she reached the far edge of the crowd, before she could make a break for her car, she heard the rising susurrus of voices: someone caught. Someone buried. A body.

Limbs.

No.

What have you done?

A cry caught in her throat.

At the edge of the crowd, farthest point away from her, three figures unnoticed by the crowd: coyote, crow, hare.

This time Ted answered on the second ring. He didn't hear the tears in her voice. He never did.

"I can't talk." His voice was rushed and frantic. She heard him fumble for something on his desk and the phone clattered down, sharp and hard. He was back an instant later. "Something's happened at the townhouses we've been doing PR for on Moana, it sounds like– yes, okay, I'm *coming*– Jen, I'll call you back–"

Gone, the silent, nothing-there of a gone call before she could say anything, Jenna's mind still reeling and no, not again, but she hated those townhouses, someone's idiotic idea to take down 50 year old cottonwoods on a vast empty lot, beautiful place that looked rural in the heart of downtown Reno, take all that beauty and slice and hack it into cookie cutter condo town homes side by side like urban nightmares and not a tree in sight.

She closed her eyes and shivered in the too-hot car, and thought of the arms that had reached up through the rubble of the admin building, body bags, fallen concrete and steel and people's lives.

And? The voice indistinct. Could be imagination, that voice, but soft, like the voices on the site of the mall, like the voices half a mile down Mt Rose where everyone still gathered around the mystery there.

And. Small voices, unheard. Small creatures, caught in the trap of too many people, too many in-fill projects and why should anyone object to utilizing a vacant lot, surely that was better than expanding even further into the desert, wasn't it good stewardship?

But there's no more water there than anywhere else, Jenna thought. *No more room. And what makes you more important than an urban raccoon, a small rabbit born in-city, a squirrel looking for a tree, not somebody's damn balcony or a federal administration building's parking lot.*

What have you *done?* the developer had demanded.

What have I done?

Why couldn't she remember his name?

She started the Honda and drove windingly, slowly, unwillingly toward Moana Lane.

The trees angled out from the roofs of the town homes, thrust gnarled, flinty branches through shattered windows, forced roofs askew. Thick with summer leaves, the trees towered even taller than she remembered, well above the two story townhouses, and they had shot upwards, fast and angry, growing before anyone could react or come to terms with the trees reappearing and get out of the way.

Bodies hung skewered and broken from the branches, impaled, bleeding. Whatever happened had happened fast, and not intentionally. The trees had simply grown, taken the space they needed, fulfilled their own needs. The handful of people killed by their need had been no more marked than a nest of rabbits in an in-fill lot a developer had a need to turn into overpriced town homes.

Jenna didn't look away. Her vision clouded and ached with the deaths and her hands curled tight around the steering wheel until it actually creaked and gave, ever so slightly, an indent of her palms and fingerprints left behind, a mystery for the police when they finished this aching, impossible day and began to wonder what had happened to the woman driving the Honda.

It took her over four hours to walk the ten miles between Moana and the crossroads at Mt Rose. She wandered through residential neighborhoods, feeling the pull of old homes, established trees towering, roses blooming, not indigenous maybe, but there long enough, no longer a shock, no longer raw upheaval.

She left the neighborhoods for the hot, tar-sticky, midday sauna of South Virginia Street, car lots, computer stores, chain restaurants, the old, not-good-enough-anymore mall and past neighborhood centers beyond it, bookstores and coffee shops, concrete and freeway exits. Further and further the city stretched beyond its boundaries, the road continuing over what had been farmland. She passed still vacant fields, dotted with For Sale signs, zoned for casinos, zoned for new money, new people. Her feet burned on asphalt. Her skin burned from greed and covetousness and maybe, sometimes, from a hint of evil.

Cars passed her, shimmering heat, exhaust visible as the sun sat high overhead in the July sky, southwest, blinding, promising, a part of what was desert, what was home.

She reached the crossroads near six. Her cell had shrilled repeatedly along the way and largely she ignored it. The calls hadn't made much sense, editors demanding stories she had never been assigned; Ted asking her to write for him, PR for the new mall; the developer calling even though he didn't have her cell number, asking over and over what she had done, what had she done, how could she, didn't she understand–?

I don't understand, she thought, not his calls or the editors or the angry people who had called to tell her she was too green, too tree hugging, people she'd never heard of, people who couldn't be calling her. And Ted. Ted calling, distracted, frantic, still at the site of the townhouses, trying to figure out what in the hell to say to media who, for a change, didn't give a damn about the PR people on site, they could *see* what was going on, they just couldn't believe it.

Ted, calling at last to ask who she was, falling away as everything was falling away, the editors, the jobs, the Honda, the house in the old tree-shaded neighborhood. Ted. The Jenna-ness of Jenna.

She walked, too hot, too exposed, stalked up the edge of the field that was no longer mall, no longer lifestyle center. The developer and his advisors, attorneys, CTO's, CEO's, CFO's, CPA's and hired merks for all she knew stood in the center of the field, voices raised, fists bunched, stringy muscles pumped. They saw her and shouted at her, the developer's voice high pitched and furious, the buzzing of a trapped wasp, and she didn't question how he knew her, didn't ask why he couldn't break free of his pack and come after her, she just walked, into blinding high afternoon sunlight. There were voices everywhere again. The police yelled after her, *Hey, lady* and *Hey, miss! Miss*! Because she couldn't walk across their crime scene, surely there were clues, she was probably transporting clues from one spot to the next on the bottom of her shoes, how dare she? Jenna walked, letting them fall behind, knowing they would stop following her as soon as she reached the far side of the field and climbed the artificial hill, somehow still there, somehow still higher than the unnatural mound the new earth had formed.

She heard the other voices, smaller voices, joyful, celebratory voices, welcoming her back, calling her back into the fold.

Entering the field felt like going home, dropping a pretense she could no longer maintain. The ground under her feet vibrated, quick shocks of electricity and energy. She'd lost her shoes during her walk, stepped out of them and kept going. If she looked at her feet, they might be torn and bleeding, and they might just be part of the desert floor. Or they might be hooves. When she tried to stretch her aching fingers out of bunched fists, they didn't open. They were hard, and dark and remained curled. Unnatural. Or natural.

She heard the voices again. Not the developers or the police. They were across the field from her now, lost in their own worlds, voices tiny insectile hums, less important than the sound of the crow's wings overhead. The voices she heard were crow and coyote and hare, voices of the desert calling her home, telling her it was all right to let go of the shape, the illusion, the dream of something else, all right to become again who she was.

The voice she wanted to hear– Ted's, calling for her, wanting her with him– was silent. Ted was back on Moana, he didn't know she was gone, wouldn't miss her until he tumbled back to their empty house late and tired, looking for her, for food, for justification.

I'm sorry, she thought. *I don't think I belong out here anymore.* Because past Ted, past the writing, past the small group of friends she'd met almost by accident, she couldn't remember anything else. Not parents, not pets, not a job or any other place she'd lived.

Instead she remembered days and nights, freezing and thawing, summer and winter. She remembered full moons and crescents, eclipses and stars, solstices and equinoxes. She remembered horses passing over the fields, and hawks and eagles and small creatures who needed her somehow, needed her in a way the people in her life never could.

She remembered guiding without violence, urging the city back and away from sacred sites, taming the shimmering violence and greed, remembered when reclamation didn't include killing the intruders.

She couldn't remember when it had all become lost, but she could guess. How long had she been with Ted, Ted faithfully representing builders, developers, economic authorities, promoting growth. He was good at what he did and she'd hoped to bring him round to the other side. She'd loved him, too, the Jenna in her had, the bit she'd allowed to slip and slide into human, the part that had forgotten where she'd come from and what she was.

Until the pain became too great and she called the desert spirits to her, called forces into play that she could no longer control, and in the process, woke herself to herself.

Go home, she thought at the developers, at the police, at the builders and reporters and the others still scattered about the field. *You're not wanted here. There's nothing left for you. I won't allow you to hurt anything else.*

Across the field the developer turned in her direction; his eyes looked inhuman. He snarled and his lips pulled back, exposing fangs in a skull face of naked greed. She recognized the ancient mask of chaos across his features, and as well the fear of the vast desert, the need to fill it all in, corral it and control it and somehow, eventually, understand it. In that instant she almost felt pity, but she recognized an ancient enemy in that face, and understood the battle yet to come.

The others surrounded her. Their voices stilled. She'd called them: they'd come. Now they'd called her, and she was here. If anyone turned and looked, now, the knot of people left milling around on the not-mall of folded, reformed desert, they'd see four figures standing on the carved-out hill: crow, coyote, hare– and big horn sheep, fitting in somewhere at last.

This story first appeared in Retro Spec: Tales of Fantasy and Nostalgia (Raven Ink, 2010) edited by Karen Romanko. Not sure where the idea itself came from — maybe my horror of trying to keep house when I can do almost anything else better?

New & Improved

She almost didn't answer the door when he rang the bell. Martha Simon wouldn't say she was addicted to her shows, but she did hate to miss what was going on. With Bill at work all day and the boys at school until he picked them up after football practice, basketball practice or baseball practice, she had nothing else to do except pick up their socks and dishes and magazines and Bill's disgusting cigar butts. She'd have loved to have a girl, someone soft and pretty and quiet to spend afternoons with.

Though if Martha was going to be honest with herself, and she might as well since no one else ever listened to her, quiet afternoons with anyone was the last thing she wanted. She had enough quiet. Half of her friends were on those fancy tri-cyclic mood elevators because of the amount of silence in their lives between the departure and return of family and the amount of mind-numbing work done in that silence. And then on the weekends between televised sports and the boy's sports, she had enough noise. She sometimes thought she'd like to try something in between extremes.

Or something altogether different.

Like those people in her shows, who were all married like Martha was but obviously it meant something else to them in Port Charles and Springfield, because they all had affairs and if they had children, those children weren't just seen and not heard, they weren't seen, either.

A commercial for laundry detergent came on and the man on the doorstep rang the bell again. Martha supposed he'd seen her through the window on his way up the walk, seen her sitting in her husband's easy chair and staring at the set. Still, she answered the door with her broom in hand as if he were interrupting her cleaning and she really needed to get back to it.

"Good afternoon, madam," he said, the first words out of any traveling salesman's mouth, unless they were "New and improved," and she was already planning her response, *No, thank you, the Ford is only two years old, a 1955, thank you, and we have all the insurance, oil, windshields, tires we need* or *My vacuum works just fine, thank you,* or, *I really don't need any more encyclopedias.*

She didn't, really. Martha was a sucker for encyclopedias and had to hide the last three sets from Bill and make up stories about what she'd spent the money on. It was just that the salesmen always talked to her about things in the books and asked her questions and made her feel so smart. They listened to her opinions and laughed at her jokes and the fliers were always brightly colored and glossy even if the resulting encyclopedias looked as if they'd been printed on newsprint with old ribbons.

The man standing on the steps in his shiny suit had been there long enough he now started to say, "Good afternoon, madam," again when Martha realized she was staring, her mouth open and brain completely inoperative. Charming.

She closed her mouth. Across the street Mrs. Turkelson twitched her curtains. *Get an eyeful, you old cow*, Martha thought, but Mrs. T was on tri-cyclics and wouldn't remember anything she'd seen five minutes from now.

I really need to get some of those pills, Martha thought and turned her attention back to the man on her porch. "What do you need?" she asked, and rattled her broom at him. *I'm busy. Can't you see I'm busy? Busy, busy, busy.*

Behind her in the living room, the show came back on. She had to force herself not to glance back over her shoulder. *That*, that was life, what was on those shows. What Martha had was a test pattern.

The salesman took a look over his shoulder, then glanced next door where Tilly Caulkins was ostentatiously shaking out a rug. He turned back to her. "Good afternoon, madam," he said for a third time. "I'm glad to catch you at home on such a beautiful afternoon."

Martha blinked. The day was scorching, early fall Southern California smoggy and muggy, but whatever. She didn't suppose honesty served door-to-door salesmen well.

In the next instant, he proved her wrong. "I need your *help*," he hissed wildly.

Martha opened her mouth to ask just what the dickens this complete stranger was talking about, and he shouted, "Get down!" launched himself at her and drove her back through the open door onto the livingroom floor.

Martha struggled up from under him just as her front steps vanished in a blinding flash. The house shook. Martha screamed and buried her head.

"What the hell are you selling?"

It was the first thing that occurred to her. Whatever it was, she didn't want any.

"You're very important," he said, without explanation,

and, "Where's your bathroom?"

Bathroom? Was he selling cleaning products? What the hell had happened to her front steps?

"*Bathroom*!" he shouted at her. "Focus, Mattie!"

Mattie? "Down the hall."

He half dragged, half pushed, shoved her into the tub as Martha heard footsteps coming toward them. She had time to see something enter the bathroom, something tall and human-shaped but with a long, twisted face like a mosquito and bulging eyes. Then the salesman turned on the water and flashed something in her eyes and Martha blinked hard – Mattie blinked hard – and she was somewhere else.

"OMG," Mattie said. "That body. Those boys. That house. Those dishes. The sheets, the dog – "

"Please," Jinx said from the controls of the time rider. "Just watching is enough."

"But I mean, I was going to. I mean, she was going to." She stopped, again, confused, and looked around the lab. Sparkling, bright, effortlessly clean, it pulsed with readouts from times spread across the boards. Almost too fast for her enhanced eyes to see, the screens lit with attacks taking place across the decades throughout the 20th century, from the flappers to the punks. Anywhere the insectile aliens thought they could get a toehold, Control had sent agents, sliding into acid-drenched hippies, ecstasy-ridden new-agers, tranquilized housewives, drunk flappers and dandies. Jinx had already turned away, bringing up 6972 Morning Glory Court where even now a team had erected deflectors and was scrubbing down the area where the stairs had been and pouring new concrete and all the while the thing blundered through the house, that cute little ranch house she had shared with Bill and the boys and Martha felt a surge of indignation that something would come in to her home and –

"You all the way back yet?" Jon asked. He'd let the shiny salesman's suit fall away. He wore the same gleaming leather body armor Mattie did.

She ran her hands over her biceps and delts, made fists and reached for the weapons array that had just slid out of the war chest cabinet. "I'm awakened. Send me back. There are *bugs* in my *house.*"

Jinx gave her a long look for that and Mattie winked. Jinx sighed.

"Jon? Going along for the ride?"

"Wouldn't miss it." He'd already shouldered two flamethrowers and a laser rifle. What did Jinx think he was going to do? Blow up Control?

The world shimmered and turned inside out and Martie had a moment to wonder what Martha thought was going on but poor anesthetized Martha with her dreams of drugs and reality of soap operas – she wouldn't remember a thing. And that seemed sad.

If she cleaned up enough this slide, she might not have to go back in that *body* again. Mattie shuddered and the shimmer cleared and she was dumped back into Martha's living room, body armor, weapons and all.

The bugs were pouring in. Jon shouted something she didn't get and they moved back to back, weapons whining as they fired up. Damned bugs kept coming and wouldn't Martha have a fit if she saw this? But maybe, Mattie thought, something about Martha just might enjoy cleaning house this way.

She pulled the trigger and a wall of flame danced out in front of her. The creatures fell back, flesh bubbling, eyes bursting. They screamed, always that mind-numbing, ripping scream that didn't sound like anything anyone could ever describe. Like death made sound. Then they charged, the flaming among them providing cover for the others, who trampled the bodies of their own to reach clawed legs at Jon and Mattie and the two of them shouted, unleashed lasers and cutting weapons.

Jon yelled, "I'm hit!" but didn't fall.

The room hadn't caught fire. This one was lucky. The creatures fell under the assault. Martha's tattered rag throw rug scorched and smoldered with bug juice. She'd wonder what had happened to it but things happened around Martha she couldn't explain. She lost time sometimes. Sometimes she had a desire for Something Else. Something different.

Something exciting.

Mattie realized she was grinning. "Martha might like this," she shouted at Jon. "I think she wanted _more_."

"They all did, sweet cakes," Jon said.

"Bite me, buttercup," she said, and "A girl likes a little fun in her days."

"I guess so."

But his voice sounded limp and as he gunned down the last of the bugs, Mattie turned her attention to the medkit, slapped a suture over the bug gash decorating his arm and did a quick X-ray for infection or poison before she turned back to the insects.

"Jinx?'

Jinx's voice held the usual time distortion through the com. "Area's clear. Looks like you two were right on top of the infestation. Good job. I can pull you out or – well, why not?"

Even as she spoke the rolled rug stuffed with burnt bug bodies shimmered and vanished.

The living room smelled funny but Mattie thought if she

opened the windows it would clear out before nightfall.

Before Boring Bill and the Belligerent Boys got home.

The fire hadn't spread. The response team had finished with the stairs. She *could* go and just the thought of being dumped into that fat, slow, doughy body again –

"Leave me here a couple days, can you, Jinx?" she asked and Jinx's voice laughed through the years.

"Always the martyr."

Martha woke mid-afternoon, mouth dry and neck aching from the odd angle her head had tilted. "Oh, my goodness." The TV had turned to cartoons while she'd slumbered half the day away, her floors unswept, her dinner unmade and – she'd missed her shows.

She sat for a minute, sad about that. Bill always said nothing happened on those shows from one week to the next that any idiot couldn't figure out without watching, but she liked them. They gave her a little bit of something different.

A glance at the clock showed her it was almost four and she got up, intending to get something to eat and start dinner and get to her chores. But outside the day was beautiful, the heat of midday calmed to afternoon golden and a small child ran by and Martha thought abruptly, *I want to do that* and got up and went down the hall to the bedroom she shared with Bill. After a long time she found a pair of cotton shorts with an elastic waist, which still fit, and a big t-shirt of Bill's she didn't think he'd miss. She had a pair of Converse shoes she'd gotten for tennis when she'd played briefly in college. She took her hair down from its chignon and put it up the way she hadn't since grade school – in a ponytail.

"What are you doing, Martha?" she asked herself when she took in her own weird reflection in the mirror.

"Something different," the Martha in the mirror grinned back, and Martha went outside.

She didn't even notice when Mattie slid out of her and went back to her own time. She'd set her sights on the rose bushes halfway down the street, ignored the niggling feeling that she ought to go spray the roses for *bugs*, get on with dinner, and then, rose bushes firmly in sight, the new and improved Martha ran.

Custody is one of my favorite story sales. It appeared in Abyss &
Apex and received a few reviews, some good, some confused. I had a
great time writing it one afternoon while sitting in the fading bright
summer sunlight outside our beat up rental house.

Custody

Daniel left that morning. He said he'd send for his things. Susan slammed the door behind him hard enough to cut off his sentence; his words bled on the floor.

"Send for your things," she said to the empty house but her words felt flat and wrong and she stopped talking and went into the kitchen to make tea and smash Daniel's favorite coffee mug.

Daniel called the next afternoon to tell her he wanted custody of the cockatoo and the goldfish. Susan told him she'd fed the goldfish to the cockatoo and then stuffed and roasted the bird. Then she hung up, ruffled Birdboy's feathers, fed the fish and went back to work.

Daniel called that night and said he wanted custody of all the house plants since she was obviously unfit to care for any living thing. Susan told him she'd burned the house plants and smoked the pampas grass and it got her stoned. Then she broke his second favorite mug, wondered about his obsession with crockery and went to bed. Since it was only eight p.m., she got up again and watched movies about people who murder their spouses until she was relaxed enough to go to sleep.

Daniel called her the next morning and told her she should expect to hear from his attorney as soon as he got one because she was obviously unfit and he wanted custody of all the stuffed animals they owned jointly. Susan told him he was insane and that the stuffed animals were now unstuffed and all their cotton fluffiness intermingled and slammed down the phone. She spent fifteen minutes crying into Mr. Bear's plush fluffiness until she could get herself pulled together and head in to her job.

Daniel called periodically over the next several days, threatening to retain lawyers and obtain writs, questioning her sanity and answering her rebuffs and eventually he called and told her had retained an attorney and that he was going to sue her for custody of herself.

Susan hung up slowly without saying a word. The only thing she could think to say was that she'd killed herself which Daniel wasn't likely to believe as long as she was talking to him on the phone. Daniel called back later that day to make arrangements for his custody of Susan and Susan, confused, went willingly.

I have no idea where the impetus for this story came from but it worries me. I don't think I ever had a little sister... I did write it for the wonderful and too-short-lived magazine Say... edited by Christopher Rowe, Gwenda Bond and Alan DeNiro, published by The Fortress of Words.

What We're Going to Do Next

This is the house the Realtor showed us. It's lemon yellow on the outside and pale cream on the inside. It looks like something you should eat, not something you should wear or drive or try on for size. It doesn't look like a house. The walls breathe. They move together in a slow dance that takes hours but it still looks like breathing. The halls don't lie flat or straight. The ceiling hangs too low, as if tired or lonely. It's a needy house that tries to get too close to you and is a little too reluctant to let go.

There's a kitchen, like in other houses. Like real houses. A kitchen and a sun porch. There's places to eat and places to fix food and under the stairs there's a deep black space to keep the unexplained bits of life. My father says it's a crawlspace, for god's sake, stop acting like a baby about it, Sarah, until I threw his favorite hammer in there and it was almost 30 seconds before we heard it hit. After that he didn't say very much about it except maybe it was a crawlspace that led into the cellar and he'd ask the Realtor or the contractor about it. In the meantime, I noticed he didn't go after his hammer.

I kept thinking about it too. Nothing I threw down there ever came back so I started tying a rope around things before I threw them in. First I threw in a piece of notebook paper and a pen but the paper came back empty. Then my mother's white board. It went in reading "bacon, lotion, dish soap" and came back blank and after that nothing would make a mark on it anymore. Finally I tried lowering my mother's tape recorder but I couldn't make out anything on the tape.

So then I threw in my little sister.

Somewhere around three o'clock that afternoon clouds started brushing away the sunlight. Katie had been hanging around and hanging around and hanging around and all I wanted was for her to leave me alone. We'd been in the house a couple weeks by then and my mother was back at work and my father had never stopped working and it was just me and Katie and the day growing darker and Katie being a pest. About the sixth time in the same minute she asked me what we were going to do next, I decided.

"Go get a piece of rope from Daddy's workshop," I told her. Daddy doesn't like anyone messing around in his workshop, which is why I told Katie to go. Anyway, he doesn't yell at Katie as much as he does at me because he always says she's too young to know better, which is another reason I hate her.

"How big?" she asked. All bright eyes. She'd be cute if she wasn't such a pain.

"The yellow one," I told her. The same one I'd been

using for everything else. Katie headed out to Daddy's shop and I went and opened the closet under the stairs. Darkness peered out. I always held on to the wall when I opened the door. Like something was going to pull me in. And I'd never stopped waiting for my eyes to adjust when I peered into that darkness and they never had. I almost felt guilty about throwing Katie in there.

She was back with the rope.

"So what are we going to do next?"

Almost guilty. Not guilty enough. I knelt in front of her and tied the rope around her waist, knotting it the way I'd learned when we tied up the row boat up at the lake. Katie's eyes got bigger. Her mouth puckered and she looked distressed. Nothing had happened yet.

"Sarah, I don't like this."

"It's nothing," I told her. "It's just a closet. Don't be such a big baby."

She sniffled at that and said, "If it's just a closet, what does it matter?" Clearly she'd figured out what we were going to do next and decided she didn't like it.

I handed her Daddy's biggest flashlight and said, "I want to know what's in there." Then I shoved her as hard as I could and the thunderstorm broke overhead. Katie screamed, either from the thunder or my pushing her or because of the closet or because of all of it, I don't know, and the rope sailed so fast through my hands I almost didn't grab the end of it in time. It pulled taut with a snap and vibrated. The weight threatened to pull me forward. I couldn't see Katie at all.

Time spun out. Rain started falling outside. I counted to 100 and then to 500 and then I called and no one answered. There was still a weight on the other end of the rope and the rope still bobbed under my hands. At 600 I started to pull her back toward me. I pulled. The rope pulled against me. The phone rang. The front door started to open. I froze. The phone rang a second time. My mother's voice said, "Sarah, for heaven's sake, answer the phone." The front door closed. The phone stopped. I gave a hard yank and Katie tumbled into my arms. Her eyes were wide. Not frightened. Just staring.

"Oh, Carol, hi," my mother said into the phone in the other room.

"Katie?" She didn't answer. I tugged her around—somehow the rope had gotten twisted about. The knot was behind her now. Her blond pony tail looked like someone had been playfully ruffling her hair. I turned her back around and said, "What's in there? What did you see?" Katie just stared, her eyes wide and round. And empty.

When she opened her mouth, nothing came out.

My mother thought Katie was playing that afternoon and she went along with it for a while. Toward evening she was just putting up with it and by the time Daddy got home she'd gotten to the "Enough is enough, young lady, I want to know what's going on" stage. Through it all Katie remained silent and when Daddy got home he scolded her and later Mother gave her a spanking. It was after that the fear started and the questions to me, had I been with her all afternoon? Had we gone anywhere? Had anything happened? I knew I could talk to them, right? With every question my parents got smaller and older. Katie never said a word. I told them, finally, that Katie had gone into the closet, but my parents didn't understand. Even my father seemed to have forgotten the thing with the hammer.

After a while I stopped talking. Because they weren't listening. I stayed home when they went with her to emergency. I stood for a long time at the edge of the closet where the unexplained things are kept. I stared into the darkness but I was never brave enough to enter.

That night my sister's ghost stood at the end of my bed and watched me sleep. I woke about three o'clock and she was standing motionless, her fingers uncurled and pointing straight down. Her eyes were wide and clear.

"What are we going to do next, Katie?" I whispered but she never answered.

This is the house the Realtor showed us. Mother, Katie and I live here. Daddy has moved to an apartment and taken all the doors off the closets. Maybe he did listen, a little. This house is chocolate brown on the outside with green trim like icing. It's not pretty but it looks like a house. Inside the walls are painted yellow and the window sills are painted different colors. The house doesn't reach for you or hang about too close: it's just a house.

There are lights in all the closets, and all of the closets are empty.

For a couple years in the early 2000s my friend Mike and I would meet regularly and do freewriting exercises until our hands cramped up and fell off. This is one of the stories that emerged from one of those 10 minute writing sprees.

Dark Streets and the Forgotten Tastes of Chocolate and Joy

Dancing Jack, wind up boy, edge of town where the harlequins hang. Mask on straight, diamonds over his eyes. Turquoise panes of paint, rhinestones glitter the arch of his brows. Dancing Jack in slicks and sleeks, tights and furs and feathers. He wears satin gloves with rings over and under and chains on his neck and between his nipples and eyeliner around his coal black eyes. He moves like a cat, he flits, he floats, he brings presents to good little girls and boys but there are precious few of those on the Dark Streets.

Dancing Jack, scat like a cat, he blends into the club, all plastic and fluid and the pretty girls and pretty boys and pretty can't quite tells, he brings presents to those and those are plentiful here. Club– slippery, sleek. Stylish and smooth. It's sliver and sleek, gold and green, it's light and dark with drinks that flame and drinks that steam and the pretty girls and boys come here, sleekly ringed, darkly tattooed. Drug patches as jewelry. Flash of silver is a med kit. Flash of chrome is a needle. No diabetics here, no, it's Jack, it's him, and he drops the packages, small squares like candies, fantastic caramels, colorful chocolates, hard candies to suck and the sun comes brighter and the stars shine harder.

She comes to him in his sleep, and always he dreams her with wings but wings clipped short, pin feathers bruised, molting, damaged. Silver wings that should tower and encase her. She dies a little in every dream and he shudders in half sleeps. In reality she died fast, so fast, she died of turquoise salt water taffy or raspberry shaped hard candy or a trace of chocolate across her tongue. She died because she danced with Jack, a pretty child took candy from his sack, sleek satin gloves tucked treats into her mouth until she choked and cried. And died. And Jack, that moment, harlequin trapped, puppet to their will, victim of his own dreams, trapped in memory, looping through life, no choice but to repeat, to bring his treats to the good little boys and girls and don't knows on the shiny side of town.

Dancing Jack, clickety clack, heels across the sidewalk and Jack in the box, Jack of all trades, Jack be nimble, Jack be quick, Jack turns tricks and hearts and quits. Jack in the box, Jack in *her* box, Jack of Hearts, of Knaves, Jack who saves.

He shoots upward in bed, mouth open in a perfect painted O, scream of negation, denial. Unmaking. He sends her away, sends her flying, he's Jack, in the beanstalk Jack, the one who wins, who runs away and lives to run another day.

The satin sheets are soaked. No denying the dream this time. He sees her again, even with his eyes open. Sees her eyes, wide and blue, and her mouth, pale and hot, the way her lips parted and she accepted the treat, took food from his hand, food of the gods, something sugary sweet and fun to eat only the fun comes after the eating and that time it didn't come at all, that time there was no after, no later, nothing more. He sits in bed, wet satin clings close, and he tries to cry but Dancing Jack is no longer a real boy and the tears won't come and when he tries to put his hands up to his eyes, to cover his face, to hide disgrace and the tears that will not come, the strings on the backs of his hands, the tops of his arms, tangle and knot and the puppetmaster pulls them tight in frustration, irritation. Jack spends the rest of the night awkwardly crumbled at the bottom of the bed where the master flung him in disgust, and the dream comes and goes for him, her eyes, her teeth. The way she died.

She slides inside. No one sees her come in. Bouncers are distracted, too many damn harlequins here, too many masks, to many masked. They have enough trouble without worrying about one lone female slipping past, doorman asleep at the switch or just not paying attention or maybe she's a ghost. Just like her sister.

Looks like one. All whites, night on the town white, stark white, snow white, death white. Long platinum hair, whitened teeth. White fur coat, white satin gloves and tights. White t-shirt, white boots. White knuckles under the black leather gloves where she holds her fists so tight they ache, holds her rage so hard it trembles.

Soon. He should be here soon. She's watched him, followed him, stalked him. Dreamed him. Hated him.

Tonight she'll kill him.

One more time she pulls the photograph out of her pocket, battered thing now, cracked around the edges as if she traveled back in time for the photo. As if she traveled forward in time for this meeting. Juncture. Connivance.

Jack. In the house. In the bar. Jack, adoring audience suspends its bacchanalia.

She follows. Through the crowd. Watches as he dispenses benevolence. This is not Jack as she imagined. A kiss here, a touch there. He cups a cheek, tweaks a nipple. He whispers in ears and they follow him, they'd follow him anywhere. Dancing Jack, treats on the tongue, magic in their mouths.

Touch me.

She shudders. And imagines her sister. And hardens.

Get away from me.

(She never had a sister.)

But he is not coming her way. Too much family resemblance, perhaps. Or something in the way she stares that frights him. He moves herky jerky, trembling limbs and strings a-tangle as if he moves to his own free will.

She thinks it is not her job to punish him. He is not the one she seeks, but the ones who pull the strings.

She will kill him anyway.

Hand on her shoulder and she spins. Him. Came up behind her. Jack in the box. Something evil this way comes. He sways toward her, lovely painted boy. He sways toward her, opens the sack of toys and *Do you want a cookie, little girl?* But he doesn't speak. She wants to touch his arms, the places where the strings or wires poke through, up close they look like wires, the way the skin pulls up and puckers around them. She wants to touch but she'd be tangled and lost, tumbled and bought, and she takes a step back to consider him coldly though her heart pounds and her breath comes quick and her thighs slacken and strain apart. She slicks her lips. She is sleek, is sex, she is this place, white on white, she has nothing to fear. Here. When she looks in his eyes she sees herself. Drowning. Over and over. Lost in the fires of harlequin eyes.

Ducks her head. Listens to her heart pound, listens to it trip. Clickety clack, the sound of Jack, back. The sound of death and sugar and joy.

He is not a real boy. She can kill him. No one will punish her for disposing of a toy. Her sister, after all, lost to night.

"You knew her." His voice is silk, butterscotch, echoes in her ears and she pulls herself closer. No one comes here if they value life. They come here looking for exit, for escape.

"I know you," he says, and frowns, because they were not just alike. She can see the dream in his eyes, smell it acrid on his skin.

"You don't know me," she says. When she opens her mouth his finger slips in. White satin darkens in her mouth. The glove is satin against her tongue.

The glove is raspberry and apple, chocolate and caramel. She can barely taste the truth under the flavors.

She sucks until there is only cloth, sodden and slick, and pulls back though Jack stands still, his hand held out to her, one finger extended, glove soaked through. He watches, impassive. She turns her gaze off him, but looks back.

"More," she says.

Jack sells dreams. Jack sells lies. All you have to do is look in his eyes. To know. Jack, is back. Under the mask, under the lies. Harlequin diamond mask, painted on. Leather mask, tied on. Tattooed. She wants to reach out and touch it. Turquoise, diamond. It glitters and glows. She reaches out and he takes her hand and she'll let him lead her, take her home. Bag of toys bumps her leg as they walk but that's all right, she's seen his eyes, once he was a real boy and can be again. She'll bring him back, sleepless nights of terror, bring him back and offer him his own Jack.

Midnight streets, slick with lust, shiny black asphalt, turquoise tights, diamond mask, a girl, white on white. Fade into night.

Clickety clack, Dancing Jack, up the stairs, without a care. What waits up there? But she is beside him, her hand in his, and it's like a dream, The dream, like the dream every night with her wide perfect painted pained O of a mouth, fish gasping dying starved for air and her eyes watching him as the room darkens around her and Jack, is back.

You're not her. You can't be her. You're someone who looks like her.

To withhold. No toys, no joy, good little girls and whats and boys. He'll keep his tights on, himself himself. No part of Jack is safe. His hands feed dreams, his legs lead to nightmares, he pumps drugs with his sex. He is a tool, a wire and string thing, a drug himself.

Her lips on his, sugar sweet, the treat he gave her earlier and he strips off the gloves, disgusted, she watches them fall, watches his face, she's so familiar, the feel of her when she sucked his fingers, his satin and silk, so familiar, the way she smells and he'll resist her, he'll send her away.

Wires pull tight. His masters know what he's thinking. They've seen it in his eyes, or the set of his mouth, or read it in the tension of the wires as he fights the configuration and pose. They know. They guess. They mean to trap the girl in white, reel her in, burn her in white flames, it's what they do to the slick and alive, the sleek and outside the norm, outside Regular Life, the ones who live and burn and turn from the true, fur and lace, slick and sleek, high heels and chains across insteps and feet, rings on nipples, chains on bellies, chests, threats. Walk away. Run away.

He cannot move. She circles him. He thinks she means to kill him and wants to feel fear. Wants to feel afraid or angry, wants to feel. Anything but empty. Anything but relieved.

She doesn't touch his mouth, painted mouth, candy apple red, dread surges through him, his mouth he could have tolerated.

She doesn't touch his mask or eyes, harlequin eyes. Surprise. She doesn't test for leather or silk or paint or pain. That he could have endured, her hands on his skin.

She touches the wires. Pulls gently. Sensation surges through him. He's hard in an instant. She gently pulls wires that emerge from his forearms, pulls his arms up, arranges him just so, a Dancing Jack, posed and flowed and ready to go. Runs her fingers over the skin where it stretches thin, puckers up around the wires. Runs her tongue after her fingers. Jack gasps. No one plays Jack. He is the consummate player. He sells and teases, taunts and pleases, gives out or holds back, he's Jack, he's the one. Not her. Not this tiny burning girl in white, so like his dream.

She opens her mouth in an O of surprise, locks eyes and holds out one finger coated in cherry juice, in pixy dust, no trust, no belief. Only relief. She slips her finger into his mouth, instantly slick against tongue and teeth, he tastes cherry and joy and chocolate and he looks again at her face and understands, suddenly, hopelessly. She is not here to kill him. She's come to make him a real boy.

The pain surges, every muscle and sinew fights the guidewires. The relief spirals away. Jack bucks like a fish on a line, like a puppet fighting free but he wants anything but that freedom. Anything is better than that. Than the knowledge freedom will give him, the memories free will would release.

The masters fight her. They jerk Jack away, tight wires, Push Her Off, Make Her Go. They want him to pick up the sack, bring Jack back, drug her, tease her, please her, beat her, beaten, bought, discarded, dead. It's what they do here on the Dark Streets. His legs jerk out, kick and flail. His arms wrench forward, and fail. To catch her. She's caught him. She holds him, slim, wraith in white, she burns and night around her steps back, picks up his sack, offers him peach and chocolate and hard candy and soft, powdered glitter rock candy off her fingers and all the while the masters fight her. She clings, to him. Not thrown, from him. Locks her legs around his. Her arms around his back. Her face so close to his. The face from the dream. He can no longer pretend. She's not dead. Somehow. Not bought and sold and fucked and led. She's her, she's hers, her own. Not thrown. She holds on tight and whispers in the night.

His name.

"Jack. Come back."

Real boy Jack, on the street. Tired, hungry, no place to sleep. Days and nights dance him, thin, tired, cold but the street has sun, he can tip his head back and see sky, clouds and daylight, lost there, face up towards air, lost in the dream of freedom.

Dark Streets closed to him now, slicks and sleeks and glitter creatures pass him without a word, without a care. No mask, no wires, no bag of tricks. They don't even see him, girls and boys and whats and ifs and lost causes and soon to be's and he can see among them those with wires, those on fire, those whose shoes clickety clack, who carry the sack and run the sweets.

Dark Streets. He waits in the shadows for just a glimpse, girl in white, wild white angel, whoever she is, she took his hand and took his life and Jack walks the streets of freedom with confusion and despair, his eyes turned inward, memory soft, thoughts of lips and touches and sugared joy, of one night of burning and the price of being his own man.

Sometimes he looks across the river and thinks of finding his masters, breaching the Dark Streets. He holds out his arms and searches for pinprick holes, closed now, no wires, no one dances Jack but Jack and sometimes he imagines holding up his arms, *Take me back.* The nights in the clubs, the lonely and the lost and the found and profound and hot greedy tongues and teeth, the way everyone came to him because he was Jack.

He wants that back.

Sometimes. And sometimes he thinks he'll leave the City. Cross the bridge, cross the water, another country altogether, somewhere he's never been. Somewhere he hasn't lost anything yet, or found it, either.

The sound of his footsteps on the street, on the stairs, in the hall. They no longer clickety clack.

But he's still Jack.

Beyond the streetlight he sees a flash of white. Of light. Of burning flame within the night, from one doorway to the next, fleet and swift. It's her. Even from this distance, it's her.

And maybe there's something on the other side. Maybe she'll welcome him back, maybe she'll take him with her when she pulls others across the Dark Streets, into the light.

Maybe she'll welcome him if he comes back.

Real Boy Jack. His footsteps carry him from the streetlight's halo and into the shine and black of the Dark Streets. Toward the clubs. Towards the girls and boys and slicks and sleeks and glitter goths and dark witches and harlequin masks and wires and toys and candy in sacks.

His feet carry him toward the shine and light and noise, and just for a moment, an instant, a breath, his shoes clickety clack. Jack's back.

Fishing Line, Feathers & Waffles was originally called, simply, Life. The idea arrived one morning while paging through the latest Spectrum: The Best in Contemporary Fantastic Art series edited by Cathy Fenner and Arnie Fenner. In the painting that sparked the story, a woman stands on a pedestal, her back to the viewer, hands reaching back to tie on wings. I made my protagonist a young girl instead of a grown woman and I was off and – flying.

Fishing Line, Feathers & Waffles

She tied the feathers together with fishing line from her father's tackle box. Her mother had always said it was the strongest stuff in the world, and complained that it got everywhere, trailed in behind her father from his shop in the back of the house. Her hands were still bloody from the feathers and she lowered the wings carefully, spreading their soft, long shapes to fit under her bed. She'd started with found feathers, but it was taking too long and when Lady Jane had come up to the back door with a freshly dead pigeon from Mrs. Hendry's coop in her mouth, it had given Bree an idea. Who would have thought it would take so very many pigeons to make one set of wings for an eight year old girl?

She could hear her father downstairs, muttering to himself and slamming doors in the kitchen. He'd be up soon to tuck her in and his breath would smell like too old fruit and his eyes would be full of tears he'd never let her see. She dropped the bedskirt over the edge of the wings and stood quickly as her father entered the room. She hoped he wouldn't see the ends of her jeans sticking out from under her nightgown. She thought he wouldn't– he seemed to miss a lot of things now.

"What'cha doing, Sabrina?" he asked. So much had changed over the last month. He never called her Bree now, always Sabrina.

"Looking for Lady Jane," she said, stepping carefully away from the bed. She didn't want to disturb the skirt or step on the wings, barely concealed beneath the edges of the pink bed ruffle. Everything in the room was pink, pink or white, except the wings, and they were gray and white and bloody.

"She's downstairs on top of the refrigerator. You want her?"

Bree shook her head. "She'll come up later."

"*You* should be in bed. Don't you know it's a school night? You'll never get any smarter if you stay up all night, mooning around looking for cats." He talked to her a lot like this. She'd never really noticed that she and her father didn't talk about anything until her mother was no longer there and then it was too late to try and fix it.

"Did you brush your teeth?" her father asked.

Bree nodded and climbed under the covers, covering up her jeans with the quilt despite the summer warmth. Her father seemed at a loss.

This is when mom always nagged me, Bree wanted to say. This is when she asked if I'd done my homework and why my clothes weren't laid out and did I really mean to wear *that* tomorrow? It's when she'd tell me all the things I should be doing and let me know I'd missed a spot when washing out the cream pitcher or that Lady Jane barfed on the rug again and she'd had to clean it up before she came up here and that was really my job, because I knew how she felt about cats in the house.

Bree looked down at her hands where they lay on top of the strawberry pink quilt. "I miss her."

Her father stopped circling the room and sat down on the edge of the bed to take her head in his hands. He kissed the tip of her nose and then held the covers up so she could slide down farther in the bed. "I do, too. I do, too." He looked for an instant like he was planning to say something more but instead he leaned down and kissed her again, this time on the cheek, and said, "Goodnight, my little angel. Your mother is watching over you with all the other angels on the mountain where they live."

Yes, but that was the problem, after all. But daddy just patted her and turned off her lamp and left the room, leaving the door open a crack so light spilled in from downstairs and Lady Jane could let herself in when she got tired of sleeping on top of the refrigerator.

"Goodnight, Sabrina. I don't know what I'd do without you," her father said softly in the hall, but not so softly that she couldn't hear him.

She heard him every night.

The house was quiet at two a.m. Her father had finally gotten to sleep, past the snoring part of the night when Bree sometimes woke to hear him through the walls, the great blowing snores that lit up the night around her. Sometimes she'd lay and listen and wait for her mother's voice to come– "Andy, please turn over, you'll wake the dead." If only. And sometimes her mother would laugh, that quiet, sparkly way she had of laughing when Bree's father was with her and no other time. She'd laugh and then Bree would hear their voices together, low and comforting, words in the night she couldn't hear but the love inside them was clear enough and she'd fall back to sleep in easy peace.

The house was quiet at two a.m., past the part of the night when her father clinked bottles together in the downstairs part of the house and paced back and forth, his heart breaking with each intake of breath, audible from the landing where she'd creep to listen, sitting huddled with the cat against her shins, listening to make sure the sighs continued and that he didn't leave her too. Listening to the silence creep into the house where silence had never been before.

Her footsteps seemed inordinately loud against the carpet in the hall. Lady Jane followed her, pouncing on the feathers where the wings were too long and the ends dragged along the floor. She'd thought to tell her father, if he woke, that she had to use the bathroom and thought to use the old one off her parents' room where her father refused to sleep, instead making do with the foldout couch in the den. But there wasn't any way to make him believe this, not when she was trailing wings longer than she was and was fully dressed, heading for the balcony of the master bedroom where her mother had been known to curl on sunny days, sipping white wine and reading romance novels with titles whose sounds slithered against Bree's ears and whose covers boasted as much pink as Bree's own bedroom.

Moonlight poured onto the carpet, through the double glass doors, and the doors opened silently, letting Bree out into the velvety air of the summer night. Overhead the moon was gently rounding and the stars looked warm and close and inviting. She didn't know exactly where it was she had to go, only that she needed to and that her heart was pounding under the t-shirt she wore.

Lady Jane pawed at the wings as Bree strapped them to her back using the belts she no longer wore, criss-crossed over her skinny chest and behind her sharp, thin shoulder blades. She fastened the last buckle and felt a little tingle as the wings met flesh as though no layer of cloth separated them. She took a breath and realized she was trembling but when she reached out experimentally, the wings stretched and gave a sudden, lazy flap that carried her to the railing of the balcony. The second stroke lifted her smoothly into the air and she had time to whisper, "Goodbye, Lady Jane," before she was winging into the night, the house growing small behind her and the moon looming far ahead.

The night air rushed over her and it was hard, far harder than she had expected, the birds always made it seem so easy, as if it were the most natural thing in the world, but Bree's shoulders throbbed after she had only been gone a few minutes.

For a little while, all she could do was try to orient herself. When she pushed upward with the wings, sometimes she shot up and sometimes she stayed in the same place. And when she pushed down, sometimes she dropped like a stone, dropping out of the night with the ground coming up at her fast. She circled the house a couple times, trying to get her bearings, get a feel for what it was she was doing. When she thought she had it, she played in the branches of the tree that stood outside her window, wove her way in and out of the evergreen. Lady Jane was sitting on the balcony rail outside her parents' old bedroom. When Bree passed the soft gray cat tilted her head back and to the side and looked at Bree in slant-eyed cat disbelief, then raised her paws as if Bree were a bird she wanted to bat out of the sky.

It was still tricky. She wavered as she went past the window and when she circled the house again, she got too close and her wings snagged against the edges. Overhead the moon came out of the clouds, a path of white light leading up ahead of her and she knew it was time to go.

She knew where, now. She'd always known, she thought. Her father told her the angels lived on a mountain and there was the mountain she could see from her window, a tall and jagged, stark mountain, capped with white even in the middle of summer. She moved around the house one more time, but she couldn't see in her father's window and she wasn't good enough yet to hover in place. She flipped past Lady Jane and went to her own window, set her sights on the distant mountain, and headed toward it, her wings taking long, powerful strokes.

The night wrapped around her as she flew. The air smelled of pomegranates and fresh mown grass and rushed against her with a soft, silky sound. The wings beat steadily and her shoulders and arms ached with a deep fire that rode her muscles, outlined their winding way through her back. She experimented with moving her legs around but they seemed not to help and sometimes to hinder, so eventually she stretched them out straight behind her and felt them go cold and stiff with lack of movement.

When the sky began to lighten and the snow atop her mountain was beginning to blush pink, she circled back toward the house. Too far, too slow. She'd have to try again. She fumbled at the balcony doors, half afraid her father would have wakened and shut them but the double glass doors still stood open, silently greeting, and Bree dropped quietly to the balcony. Lady Jane wrapped around her legs, purring in and out of her calves, while Bree reached up to remove the belts, her hands ready to catch the wings, but there as a moment's lag time before they dropped into her waiting hands and her back tingled like a sunburn where they'd touched.

"Waffles?" her father asked and when Bree didn't answer, turned to grin at her, nodding forcefully. "Waffles this morning for my sleepy angel." He patted her head and didn't ask her to pour the orange juice as he had for the last several mornings. Bree rubbed her eyes and let them close, breathing in the smell of frozen waffles toasting, a slightly chemical smell, acidic or stale, and burning.

"Dad—"

"I got 'em. You okay, Sabrina? You don't look like you slept well." He slid a plate of singled whitish squares at her and dropped into a chair across the table from her, cradling his coffee cup between his palms. Bree rubbed her eyes again and poured syrup on the waffles. Her mother's waffles had been crisp and golden with deep wells to catch the syrup and butter. Her father always forgot the butter but Bree had stopped reminding him because it made his eyes tear up. Her mother had cooked without using a recipe and now the waffles were lost.

Bree looked up and tried a smile out on her father. "Want to rent a movie tonight?" she asked before he did and watched his face relax.

By the time she'd gone a few blocks in the satiny night air, she knew she couldn't make it tonight. Her arms were too tired from the night before, her shoulders ached with a hot fire and her chest and back were sore and aching with an abraded, abused feeling. She went on another block, fighting the pain, watching the mountain that came no closer, but then she had to turn back. Lady Jane pressed close against her and Bree curled around the cat and cried quietly as she could, but her father still heard and came to sit beside her on the edge of her bed, stroking her hair and murmuring nonsense words until she fell asleep.

On the third night, her father went to therapy. He picked Bree up from her friend Jill's house after and they picked up Burger King on the way home and ate while the television played something neither of them cared about. Her father's eyes were bleak and red-rimmed and his hands shook as he poured himself a drink and settled into his chair.

"Daddy, are you all right?" Bree asked. Lady Jane was in her lap, tail lashing gently, and she started when Bree spoke, rolled over and presented her belly for scratching.

"I'm fine, angel. Just a little sad. What do you think about this show?" He gestured at the TV, a harsh blue glow, and Bree shook her head.

"I don't know," she said honestly. She'd been watching him, not the TV.

"I think the same thing," he said and lowered the sound on the remote. "How's school coming? Do report cards come out soon?"

He never knew things like that. When her mother was alive, she'd always had to point things out to him. Now he was lost, trying to do it himself. She remembered her mother filling things in for him.

"And this is our daughter–" her father would say and her mother would put in "Sabrina" and she never felt like he'd forgotten <u>her</u>, just that he'd forgotten her name for a moment. "She's going to be in the fourth– "Third" "–grade when school starts."

She smiled a little at the memory and looked over to see if her father had noticed. He was staring toward the TV with eyes that probably couldn't see it. His mouth was a line of pain against his face.

"It's okay," she said but she didn't know if she meant school or not and her father just nodded anyway.

It was very late when Bree snuck into the hall, the wings dragging softly behind her. She paused and listened at the door of the den, but her father's broken sobbing had stopped and the lost, frightening tears that followed, and all that was left was the choppy sound of his breathing, shallow and tear-filled. Bree stepped away from the door and continued to her parents' old bedroom.

The clock radio lit the bedroom with glowing red numbers. Three-thirty. She wasn't sure she had enough time. But she strapped the wings onto her back, not flinching when the tingle came. Lady Jane batted at her, swept around her ankles once in a cat embrace, and leaped to the railing to watch.

The night air met her. Buoyant, healed from the first night, she struck out toward the mountain, her arms pressing the wings up strongly and using the weight of the feathers to drop them back down for another pull. But the sky was too vast and the night was too short and she turned back unwillingly, the mountain in sight and becoming clear. She slept hard for an hour before her alarm went off and buried her head in the pillow when it did. She could still hear her mother's voice, cheerful in the morning, urging her to get up. Never because she <u>had</u> to, although she did, but because there was a great big wonderful world out there full of things she'd never done, full of lives to pick from and loves to choose amongst and decisions to make and breakfasts to eat and the sun was shining.

Her mother's voice lapsed into the silence that was

overtaking the house and Bree flooded her pillow with tears and thought about the feathers inside, gradually dampening under the cotton.

"I love you, Sabrina. Never forget."
"I love you, too, daddy. No matter what."

The sky opened around her, full of pinprick stars and a waning moon and the air had a weight to it that promised more August heat to come. Her arms were used to flying now and she craned her neck to see around her as her wings flapped and carried her ever steadily toward the mountain. Her father had gone to bed, exhausted, somewhere around ten, and his deep, rolling snores had started soon after. She had time, and she stroked hard, her wingbeats sending her through the air and to the mountain of angels.

Her feet touched down on velvet ground, warm and smooth beneath her bare toes. She had never thought to wear shoes when she flew because she had never expected to land before she returned home. Now her feet crossed the earth and she climbed the rest of the way to the meadow that lay hidden by the snow. Her feet grew cold but not as cold as she would have thought. The wings trailed behind her, scrabbling over the ground and the snow and Bree thought to unfasten them but stopped because she didn't know if it was still the belts that held the wings to her and because here they seemed right. When she thought about them they stirred and one wing brushed against her before she folded it back. A couple of the feathers looked white to her, gold tipped, almost as if they glowed, and she wanted to stop and spread them out and stare, but she was here; she went on.

The first of the angels was seated on a low bench, his eyes half closed as he plucked a desultory melody on a stringed instrument that spanned his lap. He gave Bree a half smile but his eyes seemed distant and he looked back down at his hands before she'd passed.

The second angel was painting while another chatted with her and they barely glanced at Bree at all until she approached them. Their wings, she saw, were made of iridescent feathers that caught the light and glowed. Each feather was tipped in gold and they fluttered restlessly against the angels' backs. Bree glanced at her own feathers and saw a sheen to some of them and that a couple more had been outlined in gold. The angels had broken off their conversations and were watching but with gentle expressions of disinterest.

"I'm sorry," Bree said, "but can either of you tell me where my mother is?"

"And who is your mother?" the painting angel asked. Her hands dipped brushes back to the paint and she stroked gold onto the canvas.

"Her name is Claire," Bree said, trying to think how to describe her mother.

The angel spread more paint on the canvas and Bree's mother looked from the swirl of ocher and blue.

"That's her," Bree said. Her chest was tight, like she'd swallowed too big a bite of something and couldn't quite breathe. "That's my mother." She looked away from the image forming on the canvas and the painting angel shrugged, starting her feathers rippling down the length of her spine.

"Then your mother is over there," she said, pointing with the end of her paint brush.

Bree snapped her head up. Her mother stood not far

away, wearing something light that floated about her like a spring wind and her wings coursed down her back, gold tipped and restless. Her eyes were round at the sight of her daughter but Bree could make out the laugh lines and crows feet. Her golden hair was swept back, tumbled away from her face. "Bree," she said and her voice was the same as it always was and her arms still felt as good hugging as they always had.

"I missed you so much," Bree said. She squeezed her eyes shut tight and her arms clung close to her mother. Claire dropped kisses into her hair and waited while the storm of tears ran through Bree before she gently tugged free. Bree rubbed her eyes. "I missed you so much," she said again. Her stomach was shaking as if she was scared.

Claire nodded gently, her hands still on Bree's shoulders. "I know you did." Her voice was gentle as a moonbeam, as the voice Bree sometimes imagined she heard late at night, singing a lullaby, tucking her in. "But I never left you. I've been there. I've been there all along." Her expression was calm and Bree looked away. It was the gentle smile on firm set lips that always meant her mother had decided on something and nothing was going to sway her.

"It's not the same," Bree said. Her voice sounded stubborn to her own ears.

Claire nodded. "No. It's not the same." One hand shoved a little and she reached back as Bree turned, gathering up the tips of the wings and holding them out. Bree looked over her shoulder and saw that about half the feathers were gold tipped now. She turned back to see her mother shaking her head, slowly, to herself. "You can't stay here, Bree. You have to go home. Your father needs you."

Her heart began to thump painfully against her chest and the knot in her stomach shook faster. She couldn't be sending her away. "Daddy can come here. I can show him how. He misses you, too, misses you so bad."

Claire's smile got a little wider and her eyes filled as they sometimes did when she looked out at the sunset, the mountains limned with pinks and golds and the sky shot through with beams of light. "Your father can't come here, Bree. Not now. Not yet." Her fingers twined in Bree's hair, wrapping one stand around two fingers, smoothing and tugging lightly.

"He *can*," Bree said fiercely and swiped a hand across her eyes. Didn't her mother love them anymore? Was that what happened to people when they died? They just stopped loving the people they used to love?

Claire laughed. "I still love you. You and your father. I always will. But it's not time for you to be here. You have your whole life in front of you, friends to meet, lovers to lose and find again, a husband and your own children to choose. You have school to go to and <u>have</u> you done your math homework? Your father was never very good at checking. Lady Jane needs you and your father needs you and you have so very much to do." She tightened her grip on Bree's shoulder so Bree would look up into her eyes. "Your father needs you."

Bree shut her eyes tight. "My father needs <u>you</u>," she said in a tight, hot voice that ached as it came lose from her chest. She felt Claire shaking her head, felt her give her shoulders a little squeeze.

"I know it feels like that right now. But your father is doing what he's supposed to be doing." And when Bree looked at her again, Claire laid a hand over her own chest. "He's loving me here. He's never stopped. He's keeping close all that we were and all that we had and he's waiting for the day it will come again." She paused, and gave Bree a soft smile that sent ripples of breeze through her hair. "He's doing what he can for you. He makes waffles," she said with a laugh. "He cleans Lady Jane's catbox, which is *your* job, young lady. And give him time– he'll start asking if you really intend to wear *that* to school tomorrow. And you owe him the rest. The junior high years, the fear of your fist date jitters, the fear of <u>his</u> first date jitters, the what if Sabrina hates her? fears. The warmth of the house when he comes home." She looked at Bree to see if she understood and Bree said stubbornly, "He makes *frozen* waffles."

It took a minute to look up, because she expected her mother to be angry. When she did finally meet her mother's eyes, Claire was laughing, silently, her hands on her ribs and her gold tipped feathers beating a counter-point to her silent joy.

"*You* are going to be just fine," she said and then, as if in disagreement with herself, "You have to go back," she said. Her voice was low and quiet, the way it always had been when Bree absolutely had to listen to her. "You have to go back right now."

Bree twisted her head, glimpsed her wings rising without her volition, and saw the feathers were mostly white and gold tipped now. Suddenly the turning in her stomach grew worse and she wanted her father more than she wanted to be here in this unchanging meadow with her mother.

Claire pulled her close for one more hug and Bree tried to sink the feeling of her mother's arms deep into her heart, held on until at last Claire broke the embrace and pushed her gently but firmly back.

"I will always be with you," her mother said and reached out with one finger, tapping gently on Bree's breastbone. "I will always be with you, right here." She gave Sabrina one last smile and said, "Now, fly. Fast. Go fast. Tell your father I love him and–" she paused, then leaned close to Bree and whispered something quickly in her ear. She grinned then, like she always had, and stepped back, and Bree felt home burning inside her. She raised one hand and waved, then pounded into the clear sky over the meadow and set her sights on her bedroom window.

The wings felt wrong. The edges felt barely held on by the belts, not tight, like they usually did, and once when Bree turned her head to look she saw that most of them were gold and white and a lot of them were falling away into the night blackness below. She gasped and beat harder, barely getting any lift, and looked forward again, toward home. In the distance she could see the light in her bedroom window, shining as if it were the only light on this dark night, and she set her sights on it. The air around her was warm, still, a thick and wet warmth that wanted to weigh her down, that coated the feathers and made the wings lift sluggishly and still more feathers fell lost from the fishing line, fell away into the night. Bree struggled, pulling at the air, kicking her legs like a swimmer. Her breath began to pant in and out of her lungs, aching contractions, and her eyes watered into the night wind. The night air still smelled sweet outside of the smell of her own hot panic.

She was still miles away when she started to fall and even as she tried to right herself she was sinking and her eyes were closing, exhaustion setting in. Her arms trembled and her legs spasmed and the muscles in her neck were hot and corded and tight. The ground rushed up at her and she barely found the energy to fight upward. Bree screamed and flailed against the heavy air, looked ahead and saw the light shining out of the bedroom window was not where it should be. She blinked wind-tears away and stared again. It was her father's light, in the den, blazing brighter than she'd ever seen it, and even as she watched the light seemed to grow, reaching out to touch her and gather her into its warmth, guiding her home.

As the last of the feathers fell free of the fishing line and the belts fell from her shoulders, Bree stepped over the window sill of her own room and fell endlessly toward the bed.

"Sabrina. Sabrina, wake up. Sabrina." Something cool, something wet and cool and smelling vaguely of mint came down across her forehead and Bree opened her eyes to the glare of sunlight coming into the pink room around her. She gazed for a moment at the light and then the pale pink walls and then turned and looked up at her father where he hovered, a wet cloth in one hand and the other brushing her hair back from her face.

"How do you feel?" he asked as soon as he saw her eyes open.

"I saw mom," she said, and felt the grin take over her face. She struggled to push herself upright and her father reached out for her. Lady Jane, curled at the end of the bed, looked irritated at being disturbed.

"Take it easy, Sabrina. You've been a very, very sick little girl." The room spun a little as she sat up and it had the stale smell of old fevers and sweat. She put one hand on her forehead and looked around the room. In the morning light the pink glowed like the inside of a peach. "Pink," her mother had said, wrinkling her nose. "You sure you want so much pink?"

Bree was sure and they painted the room together. It hadn't taken long before the pink did get old and she wanted to repaint it and maybe get some different curtains or a different bedspread, but by then she only had a couple more weeks and then– and then by the time she thought of it again it was too late. And when her father asked her if she wanted a change, she'd yelled at him it was all she had left of her mother and broke into tears. She gazed at the lightly pink walls and then at her father.

"Daddy, do you think maybe we could paint the walls this weekend?"

He looked surprised, then grinned. "I think we could. When you're feeling better. Sabrina–"

"I saw mom," she said, and swung her legs out from under the covers. She was still wearing the jeans and t-shirt she thought she'd been wearing. Her father didn't comment on her being dressed but he frowned at her statement.

"Sabrina–"

"It's okay." She stretched and only felt a little bit sore. "She said to tell you she loves you."

"Sabrina–"

Or was it all a dream? Because as the morning came on, she felt dizzy and unsure. And the flight was all fading and the soreness, the soreness could have come from the fever. Was it all a dream? All of it? The painting angel and the aching flight and her mother's arms around her one more time?

She dropped her toes to the carpet and encountered something soft and lacy. She looked down. Her bedroom floor was covered in feathers, soft gray and white feathers. She couldn't look away.

Her father stepped up behind her, one hand on her shoulder to steer her out of the room. "I think Lady Jane must have got a bird, don't you? I found them yesterday morning when I came in here but you were so sick, I forgot to clean them up."

"'s okay," Bree said, without taking her eyes from the feathers. There was something thin and plastic running through them, catching the light at intervals. *Fishing line. The strongest stuff in the world. It gets everywhere, trailed in by your father from his shop. Honestly. That man.* With such love in her voice.

"Don't know what kind of a bird, though," her father said, letting go of her shoulder to stoop and pluck some of the feathers up.

"Pigeon," Bree said without thinking.

"You think? Never saw pigeon feathers like this." He held out three of them to her and Bree looked silently at the feathers, their iridescent white surfaces banded at the edges with gold that shone in the fresh morning light. Her eyes pricked but at the same time she smiled and turned the smile up to her father.

"What about waffles for breakfast?" she asked and she felt better than she had in a month. "I think we're out," he said, looking about for something to do with the feathers. Finally he let them drop back with the others. Lady Jane pounced.

"I'll make them," Bree said. "I think I remember how she did them." She watched her father's face light as if the sun was glowing there, too.

"You want to cook," he said in disbelief.

"Yeah."

He was still grinning. "Your *mother's* waffles?"

"Yeah."

"Wonders never cease. You do that, I'll clean up Lady Jane's mess up here. Deal?"

"Deal."

"Question is, what's all this fishing line doing here? What do you think she was going to do with that?" He was dangling a length of it, watching as Lady Jane jumped and batted at it and he didn't seem to realize that several of the feathers were attached to it, sewn through.

Bree looked at the line in her father's hand. "Maybe she was going to make wings and fly," she suggested, watching his face.

He rolled his eyes. "*Sure*," he said. "You sure you're well enough to cook, Bree?"

She grinned at him and felt like doing a dance step right there in her sunny bedroom in the middle of all the pink and all the feathers. "I think I'm going to be just *fine*," she said and headed downstairs to start breakfast.

Jennifer Rachel Baumer lives, writes, runs and procrastinates in the Northern Nevada desert where she lives with her husband and cats in the rural North Valleys, surrounded by jackrabbits, cottontails, coyotes and quail… and possibly ghosts.

Her work can be found in genre magazines and anthologies, both virtual and print, and in the previous collection The Last Oracle & Other Ghostly Tales, available through Amazon.
She also maintains a rather hit or miss blog at
http://jenniferrbaumer.blogspot.com/

A lonely woman in a surreal city haunts her own life.
A new house in a new neighborhood reveals its ghastly secrets.
And the grimoire discovered in the local used bookstore proves to be more than just a curiosity.

How clear is the line between life and death – or between the living and the dead? What happens at the Renaissance Faire when death in the form of the Danse Macabre doesn't pass by?

In this collection of nine haunting tales, award-winning author Jennifer Rachel Baumer reveals the secrets of the dead, and the ghosts of the living.

Two young seekers looking for knowledge in the City of Answers come perilously close to dying for truth.

A woman fighting to remain sane in the face of insanity finds the cure is worse than the disease and the end doesn't always justify the means.

In two stories of sacrifice, one woman learns just how hard change is and that progress comes at a price, and a young couple have to decide if the good of the many truly outweighs the good of the few – or the family.

And in the title story, a group of friends learn just what's behind the locked door that offers questionable refuge from the rain.

In this collection of six urban horror stories, award-winning author Jennifer Rachel Baumer looks at the horror found within cities – and within the people inside them.

Jennifer Baumer — Thursdays in the Rain

A collection of urban horror

Ghosts of the Dead Ghosts of the Living

A woman on the run from an abusive marriage stumbles over gravestones for the living and renews her journey to reclaiming her lost life.

A serial killer prowls the night-dark highways, collecting souls of the living and the dead.

A misjudgment in cultural etiquette nearly spells doom for a young bride at the hands of her angry mother-in-law.

A portal between life and death disguised as a bathroom mirror leads an unhappy wife on a new journey.

A family history that foretells the future is practically writing itself. A drifter on the run from events he can't quite remember takes questionable refuge with a modern-day Dorian Gray.

In this collection of six ghostly tales, award-winning author Jennifer Rachel Baumer takes a journey into unnamed and unknown cities and the surreal darkness within them.